With You

Darya Polman

Contents

PROLOGUE   1

CHAPTER ONE; part one   7

CHAPTER ONE; part two   15

CHAPTER TWO; part one   31

CHAPTER TWO; part two   44

CHAPTER THREE; part one   61

CHAPTER THREE; part two   76

CHAPTER FOUR; part one   89

CHAPTER FOUR; part two   96

CHAPTER FIVE; part one   108

CHAPTER FIVE; part two   125

CHAPTER SIX   156

PROLOGUE

Calvin Sumner

Mom is looking at me funny, which is inhibiting the organized chaos that is packing up my whole life into boxes. Again. It feels like I just unpacked these boxes. Mostly because I had, just months ago. When I'd started looking at apartments, she questioned why I was even unpacking to begin with.

"Because mom," I had said, my tone haughty. I'd been taking a tone with her for months now, but the tone has since dropped. "I am physically incapable of living out of a box. You raised me. You should know this."

After some amount of staring, I finally go, "Just say you think this is too soon and you don't approve, so we can have the ensuing argument and I can get back to focusing on this."

She frowns. "Why do you assume I'm always going to say the worst thing?"

"I don't know. Probably because you do always say the worst thing."

"I say the honest thing. And I honestly think this is great and I'm happy for you. For you both. But can I not be sad my only son is moving out?"

"You don't think it's like not in my best interest to go from living with you to living with him?"

She looks at me questioningly. "Do you think that?"

"No," I say perfectly honest. Mainly because I don't. At all. "So I took Dres with me to look at this apartment a few months ago and he was like imagine your ideal home. And I imagined..."

"His place?"

I flush, looking down at my hands. "I just think there's a reason I didn't vibe with any of the one hundred apartments I saw. Maybe it was a sign."

"Hmm, well, just know living with someone is not easy. It's different living with family because you can get away with a lot. Living with your partner can strain the relationship if you aren't careful."

"See, now that sounded like you disapproving."

She laughs. "I'm not disapproving. I'm just saying you are not the most perfect person to live with, and I'm sure Dres isn't either. So you need to be patient and understanding and compromise. These would've been great lessons to learn dorming. In college. Which you failed to do."

"But then I would've missed out on having you as a roommate."

"Yeah because there's nothing I loved more than cleaning your vomit out of my kitchen sink."

"It was one time," I exclaim. "Look, Dres is going to be here after work and I'm supposed to have everything downstairs and ready. I've got like an hour to finish this."

She holds up her hands stepping backwards into the hall. "Okay, okay. Are you guys staying for dinner?"

"Sure," I say mostly to appease her. I grab my phone, shooting a text to Dres to let him know. He thumbs up's my message. It blows my mind that just six months ago communication between us was so poor I probably would've boomeranged my phone out the window if he'd thumbs up'd my message.

Dinner is long. Even though my mom and Dres have been cavorting behind my back for months, they're acting like this is the first time they're truly having a conversation since we moved back here. She's telling stories about California that are really not all that interesting and he's hanging on her every word. At one point I tell her Dres doesn't want to hear about how she separated twins and Dres gives me that look that's one part scolding, one part soothing.

Finally, I decide to just leave them in the kitchen swapping war stories, and start moving my boxes into Dres's truck. That's where Dres finds me a bit later, outside his truck wrestling a box past my shoulders. He looks at me with this strangely amused expression.

"You could've waited. I would've done it."

He steps forward, lifting the box the rest of the way so it's stacked on another in the bed of his truck. He does it before I can even protest, moving the weight easy. It's not all that surprising and I'll be remiss if I don't lean back and stare at him in all his muscular glory. If the younger version of me could see him now. I don't know that I would've survived working at Weston's. I probably would've resigned my first day. Forget Adonis, Dres looks like he swallowed Adonis.

Dres turns to me, staring again. There's lots of staring going on these days. My mom, him, people at the grocery store. I didn't get a tattoo on my face and forget, so I don't know what's up with all the staring.

Since it's still within my nature to make a point, I say, "I could've done it."
It's a very delayed point to make. Dres gives me a wry look. "I have muscles
now, you know. Big muscles. Muscles that can carry their own boxes."

"Oh, I'm fully aware," Dres is saying but I'm unfocused as he steps into my
space, backing me up against the side of his truck. We're on the street side
so if my mom looked out the window she wouldn't even see us. But if a car
drove by, we might end up nailed.

Totally worth it, I think as he grasps my face, tipping my head back so he
can duck down and kiss me. It's not a friendly kiss, not in the slightest, his
mouth open and wet as his tongue slips over mine.

I grip his wrists, hanging on but not moving his hands out of the way.
There was a time, so many years ago now, where we stood outside my house
like this and I begged to be kissed with this intensity, this fervor.

So I pull away, and I say, "Why Dres, you're getting ahead of yourself."

He doesn't miss a beat, smiling, as he says, "Really? Because I feel exactly
in line with myself."

We both laugh, and it's a soft sound, even combined, in the night. "Okay,"
I say after a moment. "It's freezing. Let's go say goodbye to my mom so we
can go home."

Dres pauses at that. He hasn't moved anything but his mouth off of mine.
His eyes are still closed and he nudges my nose with his. "Home?" he
repeats.

"Yeah," I say, flushing. My eyes dart along his face. He's smiling. He looks
at peace. "Home," I repeat just as he kisses me again.

When we get home, Dres parks on the street, so I take the driveway. It's
small, can only fit one car. He doesn't have a garage, either. When I get out,

I'm confused by it. Like he's reading my mind, he walks over holding one of my boxes and says, "I don't want you parking on the street."

"Why?" I ask as I walk over to get a box. He waits for me before leading the way up to the house.

"Because it's not safe. Because your cars new."

"Not safe...for my car? Or for me?"

"Both," he responds, setting down the box to unlock the front door. "I just want you to have the driveway, okay? I don't want you coming in at one in the morning and looking for street parking."

"Okay, okay," I say, placating mostly. Our first fight should not be over who's parking in the driveway. It should be over who drank the last of the milk and didn't throw out the carton. Who left old coffee beans in the grinder. Who bleached the load of darks. Who am I kidding, the answer is me in all of those scenarios.

"Listen," Dres says suddenly and he's dropped the box by the door, stepping as close as he's going to get with my box still between us. "I feel like I have to — no, like I want to give you everything? The driveway, all of my closet space, free reign in the kitchen. Uhm, maybe not that last one. But. I want you to be happy here."

I furrow my brow. "Of course I'm going to be happy. I'm with you. I don't care about driveways and closet space. We could live in a box. A box with a TV, though, preferably. I am still a video gamer — yes, yes, mock all you want."

Dres is smiling but it's small, forced. "I want this to feel like home to you. So if you want to, I don't know, rearrange furniture, or buy all new furniture, let's do it."

I step out of the way so I can put my box down and then I fling myself at Dres. He stumbles back but his arms wrap around me. "We don't need new furniture, but we do need to christen every room. As per the first commandment of Moving In Together. Deuteronomy."

"Christen every room?" he repeats back, his tone almost dismal.

I nod enthusiastically. "Starting with yours and my favorite." I wiggle my eyebrows suggestively.

"Not the kitchen," he says the same time I say, "The kitchen."

CHAPTER ONE; part one

- -

C alvin Sumner

Dres is hovering ten feet away. Sulking, really.

We haven't spoken since last night, when I came home from work and told him I was leaving. Now he's standing at the top of the stairs, watching me pack a duffle bag with that expression on his face that clearly says don't go. I don't want to go anymore than he wants me to leave, but it's the right thing to do. Which is different, I think, then his right thing. When he left, he was doing it because he thought it was what was best for me. And he hadn't even tried to talk to me about it. I was leaving because I knew it was what was best for him. And if it's best for him, then it's best for me by proxy. And anyway...

"It's not permanent," I say as I count out underwear. I have to do my laundry every night when I get home, stripping in the little entryway off of the back door before I head immediately into the basement to decon. So I won't have to bring that many with me. The less I pack, the less permanent this feels. The less permanent this feels, the easier it is to move back into my mom's place.

It's unfair, really, when I just moved in with Dres a little over two months ago. Feels like no matter how hard we try to move forward, we just simply can't catch a break. But no, that's not it. This isn't the universe trying to keep us apart. We're being smart, we're being compliant, we're heeding the warnings of this virus.

"I don't like this," he says finally. That's the most I've gotten out of him in twelve hours. When I told him I was going to move out for the time being he looked like I'd punched him in the face.

I had punched Dres in the face once and it was terrible. I didn't sleep for four nights, wrought with so much guilt about it. I don't want to hurt him. But I also will not be the reason he gets sick and dies. He's not dying. I decided that years ago. He outlives me in this life. Those are the terms and conditions of this relationship.

I stop packing, looking up and over at him. His face is all squished like he's fighting back an expression.

"And do you think I do?" I ask, getting up off of the bed to walk over to him.

He takes my hands, holding them between us. "Then don't go."

"Dres," I whine stepping close enough to drop my forehead on his chest. He lets go of my hand, reaching up to cup the back of my head. "You don't understand."

"I don't care about the risk," he says quickly.

"But I care," I say lifting my head to meet his gaze so he'll know how seriously I mean it. "If I get you sick..."

"I'll be fine."

"You don't know that." I shake my head. "This is so much worse than the President is saying it is. I mean he's literally not saying anything. But I had six patients yesterday who came into the ER and ended up in the morgue. Dres, that's insane. That kind of mortality? I've never seen anything like it."

My chest tightens just from thinking about yesterday's shift. The way we ran around trying to give everything to everyone and watching none of it work. All our treatments were for shit because the patients still died. I'm not disillusioned by medicine. I know the statistics for cardiac arrests, strokes, MIs — I know that in a lot of those instances we aren't going to be able to save them, despite all our best efforts. I know these things but it's different when an otherwise healthy, up until that moment, seemingly fine, person comes into the ER with O2 Sats in the gutter, doesn't respond to oxygen interventions, and then throws a clot from out of nowhere and dies.

I shudder, saying, "I can't save these people. I am doing everything I know how to and it's not enough. I can't save them, which means if you get it, I can't save you, either. And I'm not going to be able to live with myself, Dres. I don't care what you think you know about what I can and can't do or what I'll survive or what I'll get over. I'm telling you right now I'm just not going to be able to live with myself if I get you sick. So if you can't do it for you, do it for me. Alright? Can you do this for me? Please?"

Dres slides his hand down my back, pulling me flush against him so I have to tip my head all the way back to look at him. "Okay," he says finally, his tone resigned. "We'll quarantine separately, okay? Don't get upset. I'm going to be fine. And you're going to be fine. It's only a few weeks. We'll be okay."

He has me in his arms and it's the last time for a long time that I feel this—safe and warm in his embrace. I can say this now. We took it all for granted. The minuteness of touch. I didn't realize how much of a privilege it was to be able to hold the person I love.

Dresden Gibson

The hardest part are the days where I get to see Cas but I can't go near him.

He won't let me. Always standing at a distance, waving at me from the end of our walkway, wearing a medical mask. In March, he was bundled in a coat and then as the weeks passed and the weather got warmer, the layers stripped away but the mask remained. The distance remained.

I thought that I would get through two weeks of quarantine and then Cas would be back and everything would be right again. And for the first two weeks, I was doing pretty okay. I started working on a cookbook, just as a way to pass time. When I wasn't cooking, I was reading Cas's books. He had several boxes we'd stored in one of the closets downstairs. The house had become apparently small when Cas moved in. I needed to build a bookshelf for him (I did build him a bookshelf during week five of Quarantine) but in the meantime his books were packed away. I unearthed them and started reading.

Cas annotated a lot of his books. Maybe because they were school books and he needed the notes for essays. I didn't know, but it was more entertaining reading his thoughts in the margins then it was reading the actual book itself. Cas liked sentimental books, with lots of train of thought. He'd marked up his copy of Extremely Loud and Incredibly Close to a degree where it was actually illegible. The cover was worn, fraying at the edges. He had a few books in this condition. Ones by Palahniuk and Junot Diaz. I thought that reading Cas's books would make me feel closer to him, but I've thrown This is How You Lose Her across the room more times than I've kept count. He's going to kill me for what I've done to the binding.

So, yeah, all in all, quarantine is not going great. It was naive to think it'd be done and over in two weeks. And it feels pessimistic to think it'll never end, but most days I wake up and think this is never going to end.

Which isn't to say that sleep comes easy. It doesn't. As per Cas's orders, I have to limit my time outside as much as I can. Walk the dogs fast, he says. Always wear a mask, and cross the street to avoid people. I've been running but not as much as I probably need to now that the extent of my daily activity is walking around my 5x5 home. The pent up energy, the anxiety and fear, the longing and missing — it all keeps me up at night.

When I do fall asleep, I don't normally stay asleep for long. So it isn't all that surprising when I jolt awake one Tuesday night, Wednesday morning really since its past one. My hearts racing but I can't remember what I was dreaming about. Nothing good, I imagine.

I reach over to my nightstand for my phone. The screen blinks at me, one fifty-four the time reads. I have no new messages. It's Tuesday-Wednesday, which means Cas was working his one to one shift. I should have a text from him saying he's home. It's not a rule, but it's a rule. He's supposed to text when he gets to work and when he gets home. I consider sending a text but decide to just call instead, a hot flush of panic coating my chest. I rub at my sternum as the phone rings. It keeps ringing until it eventually goes to voicemail.

That's about all I need to be out of bed and on my feet, grabbing the first pair of pants I find. It's Cas's college sweatpants. They're high waters on me. I rush downstairs, grabbing my keys and my wallet before I yank the front door open and step outside. It's early Spring and the night is damp but still warm for April. Or maybe it's just the adrenaline fighting off the cold.

I'm in my car when Cas calls me back. I haven't even turned the ignition yet. I set the keys down, picking up the call. "What happened?" I question, my tone urgent.

Cas voice's comes over in a rush. "Uh, I'm sorry, I'm sorry. I crashed—."

"What?" I ask, my tone sharp. "Crashed?"

"I fell asleep!" he says quickly. "I mean I fell asleep, I'm sorry. I would've texted but I was just resting my eyes and then I was out. I'm sorry. Bad Cas."

"Yeah," I say taking a deep breath to calm my nerves. I rest my head on the steering wheel, closing my eyes against the rush of relief that fills me. "Bad Cas."

He laughs softly, but it's a distant thing. All of it is a distant thing now. Our whole relationship a distant thing. Everyone in my life — a distant thing. I don't get to see Jack, or Jasmine, or the kids, or Amelia, or my mother, or Olivia, or Charles, or Tasha, or Rumi, or Ms. Vivvie on Sundays, or Fiona and Antonio. Not only have I realized just how many people are in my life, and how they impact the daily function of it, but that I need that impact more than I ever thought I could.

"How are you?" I say after I've calmed down. In the beginning, I was able to fake it way easier than I can now. My how are you's used to hit a positive note. We exchanged details of our days in depth. We sounded like we would make it through this.

It's been almost exactly five weeks since Cas moved out. I've counted each day, ticking it off in my head, wondering when he'd finally be able to come home. As it stands, our county is the hardest hit in the state. They opened a Covid testing site in the community college parking lot but it's full by noon and turns away everyone after that.

Cas makes a sound. I know it well. It's the not great but don't worry sound. I am always worrying. I worry about who he'll be when this is all over, after everything he's seen, after I've sat with him on countless FaceTime calls and watched him cry, unable to console him the way I want to, unable to do anything but watch him hurt.

"All you can do," Dolores had said. "Is be there for him in any way you can. Even if it's just virtual. Even if it's through a door or a window. Just be there for him."

I want to be there for him in person. I want to hold him. I don't want to console him through a window, a closed door, a phone call.

Cas clears his throat and asks, "How are you?"

I make a sound. It's the not great but it could be worse sound. And it could be. My family is healthy, my friends are safe, and Cas has not caught this god-awful illness.

I say, "Hey, listen I'm sorry I called and woke you. I was just worried. Go back to sleep."

"No, it's okay, I'm getting ready to drive home, anyway."

I wince, gutted for whatever stupid reason. Obviously, his mom's home is just home. He's lived there most of his life, more of his life there than here with me.

"My mom's," he clarifies after a moment. "I'm sorry. I'm tired."

There's heat in the back of my throat and behind my eyes. I pinch my eyes closed, take a breath so my voice doesn't betray anything I'm feeling when I say, "Your mom's place is home, too. Be careful, okay?"

Cas is silent for too long. Then he says, "I've gotta do groceries before I come over tomorrow."

"I'll be here," I say because it's true. Because there's no where for me to go.

CHAPTER ONE; part two

C alvin Sumner

I don't sleep well these days.

Which isn't to say I have trouble falling asleep because I don't. At all. In fact, I have more of an issue staying awake. If I sit down and close my eyes, I'll be out. But my sleep doesn't feel at all replenishing. It mostly feels like I'm wasting my time because I wake up feeling just as tired as I was when I went to sleep, if not more. Maybe it's a result of the crushing fear that seems to live within me now. Maybe it's because I just want to be back in my bed with Dres.

Either way, it is and isn't a burden to be up early Wednesday morning. I don't think any amount of sleep is going to actually cure how tired I am. It makes no difference if I sleep all day or get up early. The act of dragging myself out of bed and getting dressed is still arduous. But it's a grocery day, which means it's also a Dres day. That gives me the push I need. The sooner I deliver groceries, the sooner I see Dres.

On my list are my cousins, Dolores, Dolores's neighbor and our resident Covid-Updates Blogger, Polly, Ms. Vivvie, Jack, and Tasha, one of Dres's employees. The groceries have already been ordered and filled. When I get to the store, I just have to lug all the bags to my car and then play Santa Clause with the deliveries. I do my locals first, heading to Tasha's, who lives within a few blocks of the grocery store. I leave the bags at the door of her complex building and then call her, waiting in my car till she comes down to get them. She's wearing a lime green mask and waves at me before she grabs her things and heads back inside.

From there I go to Ms. Vivvie, who lives a few blocks off of Dolores and Polly. Ms. Vivvie has an old wooden wrap-around porch with rocking chairs and a swing and tons of plotted plants. In the last four weeks, I've seen more and more potted plants show up so her porch now resembles a nursery. I leave her bags by the door, ring her doorbell and move backwards till I'm standing on the sidewalk.

Ms. Vivvie answers the door and I don't realize I'm holding my breath till she does. It's no secret Covid's been targeting and taking out older people. But Ms. Vivvie looks good, dressed in a vibrant chiffon robe. She has on a floral mask that matches the head wrap she's wearing.

"You're a godsend, Calvin," she calls to me. "You see my sign." She points at her yard. I wouldn't have noticed it if not for her pointing, considering she planted some new bushes. But in the foliage is a sign that says Thank You Covid-19 Warriors.

"That's a great sign, Ms. Vivvie," I say grinning even though she can't see it. "Stay safe."

She points at me warningly. "You stay safe."

I deliver Polly's groceries in the same fashion and then stop at Dolores's. Amelia usually gets the door. Dolores and Charles wave at me from the window in the living room, calling hello. They don't wear their masks from that distance. They look good, skin pink and healthy. No signs of cyanosis. I don't know why I think they would have that. Maybe I just can't stop seeing it now. I look at people and imagine what they'd look like entering my ER without even meaning to and then I have to force the thought away. They aren't going to get sick. I'm not going to watch them die.

Amelia's wearing a thin blue medical mask. Clinical. She's in sweats, her hair a messy bun on her head. She's sitting on the front steps when I walk up. She gives me a small wave as she calls out, "Hey!" I walk as close as I can before I drop their bags and then I back up to the sidewalk. Amelia is slow to rise and bring the groceries back up the porch. Dolores comes to the door, pulling the bags inside.

"How are you, Cas?" Dolores says from her bent over position.

"I'm good," I respond nearly screaming so she'll hear me through my mask and the distance. "Are you guys doing okay?"

"We're right as rain," she says, smiling at me as she disappears back into the house.

Amelia's eyebrows move and I think she's just rolled her eyes. "Trouble in paradise?" I ask.

"I'm losing it, Cas," she says dismally. "I wish Dres had another bed... Though I'm really about to forfeit and just pitch a tent in his backyard or something. Being back home after moving out is just..."

"You're telling me," I mumble.

She looks up at that and maybe she's frowning, I can't tell. "Ugh, I'm sorry," she says quickly. "I'm an insensitive asshole."

"What if I get like a, I don't know, blow up bed? Would you go stay with him if I did?"

Amelia's eyebrows crease. "I mean, I - I don't know that Dres really wants ..."

I nod my head vigorously. "I really think he does. And needs it, honestly. He's been alone for four weeks."

"Well then, yeah, if he's fine with it. Dolores and Charles are basically on a honeymoon. And if I have to watch another episode of Deal or No Deal I am going to go AWOL."

"Alright, I'll broach the subject with him and get back to you."

Amelia stands, wiping the back of her sweatpants. "You don't think you're going to be able to move back in anytime soon?"

I shrug, disheartened. "I have no idea, honestly. The numbers are still rising. ICU's full. ER is taking the overflow. I don't think there's an actual moment during my shift where I don't cross Covid's path."

"Damn, okay," Amelia responds. "I'm happy to do it if he wants me to. But you know what he really needs is you, right?"

"I do, yeah," I say quietly, not really concerned if she hears me or not.

There was a time in my life where hearing something like that would've sent me over the moon. It's not a question anymore, of Dres needing me. I think the last eight months have proved as much. I need him just as much, if not more. And the moment, the second, it's safe enough to go home to him, I will. Until then, this is the best I can do.

"I'll text you," I call to her.

When I get to Jack's, he's standing outside on his phone. I step out, walking to the middle of his front path, where I drop his bags and then wait for him to finish his call on the sidewalk. He's wearing basketball shorts and slippers with a button up and tie. He doesn't have a mask on and gives me a sheepish look as he tucks his phone into his pocket and walks out to get his groceries.

"The lifesaver himself," he greets with a small smile. "Sorry bout that. Dealing with about a million things here."

On his front lawn is a sign that says Honk! An Amazing Teacher Lives Here. Jasmine teaches grade school, fifth grade. I can't imagine how hard online schooling must be and with their own kids at home. I understand why Jack's looking a little worse for wear.

"How are you?" he asks. He hasn't backed up that much and I'm uncomfortable with the lack of space between us, even though it's at least six feet of distance.

"You know," I say with a shrug.

Jack raises an eyebrow questioningly. "No, I don't know. S'why I asked."

"Are you gonna run back and tell Dres? He's worrying enough as it is," I say after a moment. Maybe that's a bit pointed but I'm not in the business of mincing words at the moment, a side effect of being absolutely bone-weary.

Jack laughs at that. "No, your secrets safe with me."

I shrug and nod at the same time. I'll take his word for it, I suppose. "Well than in that case I'm absolutely shit. I honestly feel like a newborn baby? Because all I wanna do is cry. About literally everything. Cry because I'm tired, cry because I'm angry, cry because it feels like there's no end in sight here, and our government is shit, and this situation is shit, and am I ever going to be within less than six feet of Dres again?"

Jack is looking at me a little wide-eyed.

I rub the side of my face, taking what I hope is a calming breath. "Fuck, I'm sorry."

"No, no you just answered my question. I had a feeling you were bottling some shit in," Jack responds quickly. "I know this is hard, Cas. And even saying that I'll never really know it the way you know it. The way you're seeing it. But you can't keep all that stuff inside of you. You look like you're ready to implode."

"Yeah, but I don't want Dres to..." To what exactly, I don't know. Worry? Do something stupid like break quarantine? That last one, I think. I can't stop him from worrying but I can keep him safe.

"Dres can handle it," Jack says. "You don't need to tiptoe around him."

"He already feels helpless being stuck in the house. I don't want to give him a reason to break quarantine."

"He's more likely to break it if he thinks you're hiding stuff than if you just tell him that things suck right now and you're not okay. You're both pretending like it's all fine and dandy and it isn't."

I furrow my brow. "What do you mean he's pretending?"

Jack falters for a second, looking like he's thinking over what he's said. "Uhm."

"Did he say something to you?" I ask. Because he hadn't said anything to me. Dres has been aloof, at best. He sits on our FaceTimes and nods and listens to me vent about patients, about people not taking the mask-wearing seriously, about people who come in thinking they're going to be fine and leave in a body bag. He listens and he says nothing about what's going on with him and I'm the idiot that just lets him, fuck.

"Look, if I'm not going to tell him what you just said then I really can't tell you anything he's said. Just talk to each other, okay? Communication is your only life line with him at this point."

I rub at my eyebrow, feeling a headache coming on. "Yeah, okay, you're right. I gotta head out and get the last of these groceries done so I can get to his place."

Our place. Fuck. This pandemic absolutely blows.

Dresden Gibson

Cas is late and I know I shouldn't be mad but I am.

Days like today are the closest we have to normalcy. This is the only time where our relationship gets to exceed telecommunication. I can't really justify being angry, though, when he's out delivering other people's groceries in the middle of a pandemic, after working a full twelve hour shift saving people's lives and exposing himself to this disease. I feel like absolute shit about it.

But I'm still angry.

I know the anger is really just me missing him. I do, logically. I've had this conversation with Ashley during our telemedicine sessions. Fear can manifest differently for everyone, and it can manifest differently for you every single time you face it. There are some days where my fear shows up as a symptom. My stomach will churn acid all day and I won't be able to keep any meals down. When I was watching the news and reading articles and the tweets (Cas made me a twitter), I would get all hot and itchy and my skin would be covered in hives like I was actually allergic to the facts of this pandemic. I've started avoiding the news now.

It's late afternoon when Cas texts that he's here. I rush for the door, pulling it open. He's standing a few steps back from the bottom of the stairs which is the closest he's gotten in a while. There are four freezer bags outside the screen door.

"You should put those away real quick," he says, his voice muffled by the mask. I hear him but I'm not really focused as I try to absorb him at the same time. He looks drowsy, his eyes droopy and low. He's only in jeans and sweatshirt, no jacket, but it's warm today, sixties, and warmer in the sun. Today would've been a nice day for a hike.

"Dres?" Cas says after a moment.

"Right, yeah." I push the screen door open and slide the bags inside. "I'll be a second."

"Take your time," he responds and it's too casual, making me suspicious. Cas hasn't moved his hands from behind his back, rocking on his feet.

I bring the bags into the kitchen, wondering what he's up to. I'm quick to put the groceries away, shoving everything that needs to be refrigerated onto the shelves. I can organize them later but I've got a limited amount of time with Cas and I'm not wasting it.

When I get back to the door, there's a bluetooth speaker siting on the top stair. Cas is looking down at his phone. "What's this?" I ask and he jumps.

"Oh, shit, that was fast. Wait one sec, one sec." He hits something on his phone and music starts playing. At first, I don't recognize what it is. Until Marvin Gaye's voice comes through. I know this song well but what I'm wondering is how Cas knows this song. I'm confused what's happening until Cas starts dancing.

Calvin Sumner

I am dancing publicly for this fool that is how much I love him.

Dresden Gibson

"You're not going to let me dance alone, are you?"

"Cas," I say slowly, unsure what I'm evening trying to say.

"Dance with me, big guy."

Cas's eyes are shining and in the sunlight like this, it hurts to look at him. It hurts to not be able to close the distance between us, take him into my arms, and sway to the music. He's right, though. I'm not going to let him dance alone. Not when he's asking like that and the closest he's been in w eeks.

I start moving, shaking my shoulders to the beat. Cas has his hands in the air, but not completely. They're in line with his shoulders and he's moving his hips side to side. It's the most on-beat I've ever seen him dance, like he's been practicing.

"You're better at this than I remember," I say after a few songs. Cas is panting a bit, crouches and then just takes a seat at the bottom of the stairs.

"I took a dance class," he says between big breaths. The mask gets sucked into the hollow of his mouth and then blows out like a bubble. "How did I get so out of shape in four weeks? I want a refund."

I sit down on the floor. There's a screen door, four steps, and the length of the front stoop between us. "You took a dance class?" I ask.

"Yeah, college. My last year. I had met my requirements so I decided to take a blow off class. Naturally I was the comedic relief for everyone."

"Naturally," I say grinning.

Cas turns, pressing his back against the banister so he's lying across the stair. I turn and sit back against the doorframe so we're at different ends. I want to ask him to take the mask off but I know he won't.

"Can I say something?" Cas asks after a moment of silence.

I nod my head. Cas is quiet. Then he says, "When this is all over, like really over, I want to go away, I think."

I hum thoughtfully. "Go away where?"

Cas looks up into the sun, closing his eyes as the rays warm his skin. "Europe. But I'm not talking like four days away. I'm talking a whole summer."

"Okay, so we'll go away for a whole summer," I respond simply.

Cas opens his eyes at that, looking over at me like he's wondering if I'm bluffing or not.

"We could start in London," I say. "Stay for a few nights. And then we'll go t o..."

"Brussels," he says excitedly. "I have always wondered what the hell is going on in Brussels. Do they eat brussel sprouts there? Or absolutely hate even the suggestion of it? Brussel sprouts? How tourist, how gauche."

I laugh quietly. "Okay, Brussels. And then from there we could probably take a shuttle down to Paris."

"Paris, yes, yes. I love that for us. And since we're already in France, we might as well go to Cannes. Probably would only need a day there. And then!" Cas stops dramatically. I wait. "Italy."

I nod enthusiastically. "Milan, maybe. Definitely Bologna. Venice. The Amalfi coast."

"All of it. Add it all to our itinerary. Florence, Pisa, Rome. Go big or go home, right?"

"So then why stop at Italy? We'll go to Spain next. Barcelona and then Madrid. You'll love it."

"You've been?" he asks.

"When I was, I don't know, thirteen maybe fourteen? Dolores's family lives in Valencia."

"Are they still there?" he asks and I nod. "Great, then Valencia, too."

"Portugal's right there. A hop skip and jump to Lisbon."

Cas's eyes are pinched, the only indication I have that he's smiling. "Are we getting predictable with this trip? I would hate for us to be like every other tourist." He says tourist like it's an absolute insult.

"We'll throw something unconventional in, then. I don't know...." I'm imagining a map of Europe, trying to decide where we could go from Lisbon that would make sense.

"Morocco," he says quickly. "What about Morocco?"

"I think Fester would want us to visit Fes," I say cheekily.

"Fester would demand it of us. Add it to the list."

"We'd need something relaxing to end the trip with — an island." I think for a moment before saying, the same time Cas does, "Greece."

"Wow, look at us. So simpatico," Cas says with a laugh. "Cas and Dres take Europe. Light at the end of this freaking tunnel."

I pause at that, staring at him curiously. He's hard to read in a mask. "How are you doing? Really?"

Cas looks over at me at the question, surprise in his eyes. He clears his throat. "I think it's stupid that we try to spare each other's feelings."

I tilt my head questioningly. "What?"

"Jack told me you've been pretending that everything's fine?"

I fight back the urge to make a comment about Jack involving himself when he has no right to because what he's said isn't untrue and honestly, Cas is right too. It benefits no one if we can't talk about what's really going on

"So yeah," Cas says when I don't immediately respond. "I think we can just say that things suck and this isn't easy and I fucking miss you. A lot. Even though you're literally six feet away from me."

Calvin Sumner

Dres's expression opens. He says, "You don't have to be six feet away, Cas."

I frown. He can't tell that I'm frowning though. I'm wearing my mask. "Yes, I do."

"What would you do," he says slowly. "If I just opened the door—"

"Stop," I say quickly, interrupting him. "That's not an option."

"I mean, it is an option. It's just not one you approve of."

I sigh. "I told Jack this is why I don't say anything to you. Just because I'm sad and I'm scared and I'm frustrated, doesn't mean — I don't want you to do something drastic, okay? I get that this is just how I'm going to feel for a while. It's all worth it because at least I know you're safe."

Dres looks away, dropping his head so he's staring at the floor. "Yeah but what about me?" Before I can ask what about him, he goes, "I worry about you. All the time. I wake up worrying about you, I go to bed worrying about you. I watch the news and I worry about you. I don't watch the news and I still worry about you. I hear these horror stories about the PPE shortages, people wearing the same masks for weeks, doctors having to intubate without any PPE..."

He tips his head back and it thuds against the door frame, this soft sound as he gets quiet. His head tilts my way after a moment. His eyes are glassy. "I just worry about you."

I don't know what to say. He should worry, I think. This is the most unprecedented situation and my hospital is at capacity and I'm exposed to Covid every single day. There isn't anything I can say that changes these facts.

So I say, "Well I'm not dying any time soon. I'm not done with you just yet."

"Oh, you're not, are you?" His tone is flirty. Good. We can drop this then.

"Uh uh," I respond. "For starters, there are seven countries we're going to bang in. It's on the bucket list now, which means we have to do it."

Dres is smiling. "What else is on this bucket list?"

"Marriage," I say before I've even thought about it. It's too late to take it back now and if I've frightened Dres, his expression isn't letting on. The silence weighs on us.

"Kids?" he asks finally.

I breathe a laugh, relieved. "Kids are definitely on the bucket list."

"So then we'll need to get a bigger house," he says.

I groan. "That'll be your job, big guy. I cannot go through another bout of real estate shopping."

"It'll need to have a pool," he says. "And I think I'd like a place with a farmhouse kitchen."

"I have no idea what a farmhouse kitchen is but I am down if it means we can have chickens," I say grinning.

"You have no idea how to raise chickens," he says.

"I'll learn obviously! Why does everyone claim to love me but always denies me the pets I want?"

"Chickens aren't pets."

"They could be. I'd put collars on them. I'd walk them around our back-yard. I could even teach them to swim."

"I am concerned by all of what you've just said. How about a cat?"

"A cat is not a chicken, Dres," I say haughtily.

Dres rolls his eyes. "That's kinda the point."

Dresden Gibson

Cas is falling asleep on the stair.

Admittedly, I'm letting him because I'm content to watch him sleep. But I know he's tired and he has work tomorrow so I finally say, "Cas." But he doesn't budge at that. "Babe, wake up."

His eyes jolt open. "Babe?" he says loudly like he was not just fully asleep. "Did you just call me babe?"

I did, mostly because I knew it'd get his attention.

"Come on," I say ignoring the face he's giving me. "Go home and get some sleep."

He raises his hands into the space between us, clenching at the air. "I could strangle you right now, Dresden Gibson. Calling me babe when I can't even get near you. Un-freaking-believable."

I raise an eyebrow questioningly. I can't cut the amusement out of my voice. "I didn't call you babe to turn you on, Cas. It's not my fault literally anything gets you going."

"Yeah well if this was your ploy to get me to break the six feet rule, it's not going to work. I once edged for a whole month. I am a pillar of self control."

"I was just trying to wake you up," I say innocently, because I am innocent. I can't get edged for a month out of my head. This kids going to be the death of me. A thousand little deaths.

"Likely story," Cas says as he stands. He stretches his arms over his head and his sweater rises, revealing this sliver of skin above the line of his jeans. I drink it in because it's all I get, peaks of skin, memories of touch. "Alright, I was kinda saving the best for last. Well, for the sun to go down actually cause I thought that would be more romantic. In my search for some dance music, I came across this song and I was like wow, okay, this is perfection and so this is my dedication to you."

"Wait what?" I ask but Cas is already turning the song on. It's The Spinners. Cas snaps his fingers, swinging side-to-side. As the chorus starts, he makes a fist, holding it to his mouth as he sings. "Whenever you call me, I'll be there. Whenever you want me, I'll be there. Whenever you need me, I'll be there."

I sing the next verse, quietly at first and then louder. Cas shakes his head. "Of course you know this song."

"It's a great song," I say fondly.

"It is," he admits, shaking his shoulders on beat. "It makes me think of us."

When the song ends, I say, "It makes me feel hopeful."

CHAPTER TWO; part one

C alvin Sumner

I miss Dres.

But, I also really miss Dres's dick.

Which he is stingy with. Like he was stingy with it before quarantine, and I can't help thinking that if he had just, you know, let me get my fill, this would be easier. But alas, here I am, utterly dick-deprived.

It's been five weeks since I moved back home with my mom. She and I work on opposite schedules. It's purposeful as to lower the risk of cross exposure. So I've just gotten home from a night shift when she's heading out the door, leaving me with the house to myself for the next twelve hours. It's lonelier like this, but also safer.

Three days into quarantine, we had this huge, monumental fight. I'd just come off of a double, had seen enough patients that I wasn't even seeing properly and pronounced more patients than I had in my entire career. I wanted my mom out of this. I was ready to move into a hotel for the rest of the pandemic, but she flat out refused to be sidelined. I pulled out a three tier argument, starting with logic ("think of your age, mom"), then with non-logic ("if something happens to you, you'll never get to see me grow up"), and then flat out desperation ("please, please, please, please.")

It felt like I was constantly fighting with the people I loved to keep them safe, which was supremely freaking annoying. And exhausting.

Mom won the argument, needless to say. The way she always does.

"Calvin, I have no risk factors. I'm completely healthy. And my patients are pregnant moms not covid-positive emergencies. We're not even allowing family in delivery. And everyone's wearing masks. I have very little exposure. You, on the other hand..."

She was right, of course. Which was why I said I'd move into a hotel, then, to reduce her risk of exposure from me. Which only further escalated the argument. She straight up body blocked the exit and wouldn't let me leave. Because what if something happened to me? Nothing's going to happen to me even if I do catch Covid and chances of that occurring are high and very likely. But I'm young, active, healthy. I'd likely be fine.

"Likely isn't definitely," she'd said. "The coronavirus is a valkyrie. Do you understand what I mean when I say that?"

"Uhm, no, should I? What the freak is a Valkyrie..."

"I mean it chooses who lives and dies without reason, like a whim. You've seen healthy and unhealthy, young and old succumb to this disease. So don't be reckless."

"I'm not reckless. I'm trying to keep you safe."

"I've lived a long, fulfilling life Calvin. You, on the other hand — your life is just beginning. So maybe if someone needs to sit this one out..." She'd shrugged.

It wasn't like the thought hadn't crossed my mind. I could be at home with Dres, in the sexiest, steamiest quarantine of my life. Stuck in a five by five space with absolutely no interruptions, no distractions, only Dres? Sign me up.

That wasn't real life, though. I took an oath and I owed it to my colleagues, at the very least, to stay and help fight this battle with them.

We came to an agreement eventually. Socially distanced living arrangements, opposite work schedules, minimal interaction. A different type of quarantine. A safer one, but a sadder one, too. You genuinely do not realize how much you'll miss interacting with people until you have to stop interacting with them, at least in person.

You would think with all that's going on, all of the stress and exhaustion, I'd be lights-tf-out in t-minus five, but after I've decon'd and crawled into bed, I'm unable to shut my brain off. It's running its own marathon, a leg still in the ER thinking about magical cocktails of medications we haven't tried yet, anything that could help, that could postpone death just a little bit longer, something that will help people hold on.

I've got another leg stuck in a memory, a good one, one where I'm at home with Dres and coronavirus is this stray comment on the evening news that nobody's paying attention to, not when Dres is lying between my legs and his hands up my shirt and I feel like I've just won the lottery, I feel like eighteen year old me stealing kisses in the hallway of Weston's as I'm about to clock in.

And then there's my arms, deadweight, stuck here in this bed, restless. That's when I recognize the feeling for what it is. Maybe it's not just restlessness, but maybe I can ignore it.

I manage about six minutes of trying before I make the decision to Face-Time Dres. Since he has me check in before work and when I get home, I know he's up. He answers my FaceTime nearly immediately. I try not to preen, but I'm preening just a little bit. He always answers my calls on the first ring. Makes a dude feel special.

"Morning hot stuff," I say as I prop my phone up at the edge of my bed against one of the pillows.

"Hey," he says distractedly. He's in the kitchen, and half in the frame so I can see the stove and the window above it. It's sunny outside. I think we're hitting high seventies today. It'd be a great day to take a drive.

He steps into the camera, leaning on the counter so all I can see are his shoulders and face. Nice shoulders, nice face. I am certainly not complaining. He quirks an eyebrow. "What are you still doing up?"

I'd amazon'd Dres a phone stand because on Day 8 of Quarantine, he dropped his phone so many times during our FaceTime he put a crack up the side. Now all he does is grumble that his thumb gets cut on his screen.

I'm about to tread some deep ass waters. I have to go slow. So naturally, I start the way any good ask starts. I give him my best doe-eyed face. "You love me, right?"

His eyebrows meet on his forehead. "Why are you — what, what's going on?" he asks slowly, confused.

"Would you do anything for me?"

His confusion turns to suspicion in an instance. "Depends," he says after a beat. "What do you want?"

I keep my tone level. Clinical, almost. "Show me your dick."

His expression breaks and he's smiling but it's a small thing. He may also be blushing a bit. "What, why?"

That is not a no, which means we are nearly in business here. "Because reasons," I answer quickly.

He lowers his jaw into the palm of his hand, resting it there. "Reasons like sexual reasons?"

My face gets hot, which is kind of stupid considering everything. FaceTime sex wouldn't even be the most explicit thing Dres and I have done at this point. "Yes, Dres, sexual reasons."

Dres's expression is thoughtful, like he's weighing the pros and cons. He taps at his cheek as he thinks. "Well," he says finally. "What do I get in return?"

"What?" I nearly scream. I went into this call with a half-chub already and the teasing tone Dres has suddenly taken has me on a quick path to fully hard.

He raises one eyebrow, smirking at me. "If I show you my dick, what are you going to do for me?"

I flail and my phone falls over. Dres goes, "Cas?" I take a deep breath. I'm definitely hard now.

I right my phone, saying, "There was a fly."

His expression is coquettish, I think. No, yeah, definitely coquettish. "A big fly, I'm guessing." And that tone, don't even get me started on that tone. I realize I may actually be completely gone on sexual frustration now because the look he's giving me and the way his voice has lowered, it's all doing things for me. Or to me. To and for me, I think.

"This a turn of events I was not expecting but I am also here for," I say shifting because my dick needs to breathe. I need to breathe, honestly, cause I'm definitely not right now.

Dres laughs quietly. "It's a turn of events that took longer than I expected, honestly. I had money on week two of quarantine."

I gawk. Two weeks? Does he think I'm some sort of animal. "I'll have you know I'm perfectly capable of sexual restraint."

"Ah, right, the month of edging," he says, amusedly.

"Exactly. Pillar of restraint over here. Pay some respect on my name."

Dres blinks at me but it's like an intentional blink. A disbelieving blink, if you will. "Well, should we keep this string of restraint going then?"

"Dres," I say, aghast. "My dick is so hard I could probably put up wood with it. I don't even know. There's actually no blood in my brain because it's all in my dick right now."

Dres is laughing at me and it's actually not funny. Can you be sexually backed up? I think you can. It sounds like science. And I'm a doctor, I'd k now.

"Stop pouting," Dres says after he's done laughing. "I'm in. Let's do it."

"You are?" I can't keep the shock out of my voice. And I'm suddenly remembering that thing Dres said once about the gift horse.

Dres rolls his eyes, but it's playful. "Get your dick out before I change my mind."

"Literally don't have to tell me twice."

Dresden Gibson

Cas's dick is on my phone screen.

For all intents and purposes, I am trying not to think about it because if I think about it, it makes me a little crazy. If I'm functioning on crazy, then I'm not functioning on logic. And logically I know that I cannot get into my car and go over there. Even though I desperately want to. So I'm both thinking about it and not thinking about it and looking at it and not looking at it.

There's no reason the iPhone camera quality should be this detailed.

It feels like I'm in Cas's room with him, lying beside him in bed. I've imagined watching Cas touch himself before. I always fantasized that he'd move slow, drawing it out, teasing himself, matching his pace to his soft pants. He's not moving slowly, now. He keeps his hand at the tip and fucks upwards into his fist, these fast, uncontrolled movements. I keep forgetting I have my own dick in my hand and that I'm not actually supposed to be watching because I can't stop watching. Cas marvels me.

If I were in bed with him now, I'd hold back from touching him as long as I could but it wouldn't be all that long. Even my control knows it's bounds and will not hesitate to exceed them. And then I'd lean over, kissing his collarbone to start, licking at the hollow space above it. I'd suck his Adam's apple into my mouth, tongue pressed flat against it so I could feel it lift when he swallowed, catch the vibrations against my teeth as he moaned. I'd rest my head on his chest, drag my fingers along his hips, until I'd eventually reach over and join his hand.

But I'm not in bed with him. I'm here, sitting on my counter, which is not the most ideal location for this. Cas wasted no time undressing and once his pants came off I didn't have it in me to relocate. He was already hard, didn't even need any lubrication to start, but that's always been Cas. It makes me wonder what he'll be like in another five years or twenty-five. If we'll be seventy, breaking hips in bed.

Cas has requested I take off my shirt because "I gotta see dem abs" as he puts it. And then he's all surly, saying, "How do you still have abs when you've been out of the gym for weeks? This is unfair."

I still have abs because all I've been doing at home is CrossFit workouts that are chipping away at my muscle like a hacksaw. I've literally never seen weight shed off my body so fast. Cardio is cutting down all the lean mass I'd worked to gain. Kind of absurd that five years of training can disappear in five weeks. I didn't even want to think about what my bench was going to look like when I eventually got back into the gym.

I'm too in my head and by the looks of it Cas isn't going to last very long. I lean back on my left arm, tilting my head so I can watch my phone screen. Cas's chin is tucked against his chest. He's looking down at his phone and his hips have started thrusting off the bed so I know he's close. I match his pace. It's getting more vigorous as the seconds pass. Cas bites into his lip when he finishes, spilling over his knuckles. It's very quiet for Cas. I follow nearly at the same time. It feels like the kind of release that offers little actual release.

I'm reaching for a napkin beside me when Cas makes this sound and I know it. I've heard it before. I turn back to my phone. Cas has thrown his arm across his face and his shoulders are shaking as he cries.

"Ah, fuck, fuck no. This wasn't supposed to — fuck, I'm sorry. No, this was supposed to be good for us. Fuck." Cas is moving before I can even think of what to say, hanging up the call without ceremony.

Cas hanging up on me is not a thing that happens all that often, or ever, really. So it takes me a moment to catch up with everything that's just occurred. I've got post-orgasm fog and the general confusion of the turn of events to work against. When it does finally register that Cas just hung up on me, I'm annoyed and angrily call him back. He doesn't pick up immediately, which serves to agitate me more.

I'm back on the floor, tugging my pants on and Cas has moved his phone up close. He's lying down again, his face mostly turned into his pillow.

"Sorry," he says after a moment, his voice raw. "That was not — that's not what I wanted to happen. I don't even know — like, I'm okay, so I don't know why that just happened."

"You hung up on me," I say sort of stilted.

"I didn't want you to see that," he says quietly. "Can we just pretend that didn't happen?"

I frown. "No, no we cannot just pretend that didn't happen. Talk to me."

He looks like he's going to cry again, which is not what I want. That is the opposite of what I want. And that small thread, that little bit of sanity left in me is trembling and weak and I just want to get into my car and go over there.

"I just, I'm like overwhelmed with missing you."

He gives me exactly zero seconds to respond to that, swiping at his cheeks again as he laughs nervously. "Which is crazy right. Like I've gone a whole five years without you. This doesn't make any sense. Just ignore me."

"Please stop writing yourself off," I say quickly. "You're not — you're not alone in this, Cas. I'm wrecked. I'm wrecked every day without you. So if you feel like you're the only one who's overwhelmed, here, well, you're wr ong."

Cas is crying again. It's the kind of crying that hurts to watch, hurts to hear, loud sobs and snot coming down his face. I can't stand it, so I'm moving before I've even made the decision at all, grabbing my keys, getting as far as the walkway before Cas stops, staring at me all glassy and red-rimmed eyes.

"You realize you're outside without your shirt, right?" he says.

I halt, glancing down at myself.

"I mean," he continues. "I love for the world to see what I'm working with but you know that one neighbor of yours is like super conservative Christian bible thumper. Public indecency may send her into cardiac arrest. And where are you even going?"

My expression feels like a giveaway but I can't fix that as I'm too busy getting myself back inside. I don't have shoes on, either.

Cas has paused, staring at me inquisitively. "Oh my god, were you going to come over here? Dres, you can't just — you cannot. No. Just no."

"Cas, this whole thing is stupid. We can put an end to it any time we want. Like right now. Just come home."

He's quieted and I think, I hope, that he's considering it. That he's weighing the risks, the pros and cons, and he's going to rule this in my favor. I go back to the kitchen, setting my phone down on the stand as I wait for his response.

"Say you miss me," he says after a moment.

Confused, I say, "I miss you."

"And say you love me."

"Cas," I say instead because this is stupid.

"Just say it. Please."

"Of course I love you," I say.

He takes a breath. "Okay, I'm okay."

I heave my own breath, loudly, leaning over to rest my head the counter. The stone is cold. It feels good. "Well I'm not," I mumble but it's soft enough that he doesn't hear me.

"Dres," Cas says so I sit up to look at him. "I'm sorry I ruined it."

"You didn't ruin it," I say quickly.

"The first time I get your dick on my phone and I cry, like come on."

"You didn't ruin it," I repeat.

"I feel like, I don't know. I miss, you know, intimacy between us but I also just miss eating breakfast with you and sleeping in the same bed and our lives. I just miss our lives very much."

I want to say that we'll have them back eventually but I don't, because he knows that and it isn't helpful. Eventually is a non-answer, its pie in the sky.

"Why don't you go to sleep," I say finally. "And I'll stay on the phone."

He squints at me, and he's smiling a bit. I'd like him to be smiling more but I'll take it. "What? We can't. Our phones will die and like, that's a long time to keep a FaceTime running."

"Your chargers right there next to your bed. Plug in your phone. Go to sleep. I'll be here when you wake up."

He nods. "Okay." He sits up, reaching behind his phone. He's upside down for a moment before he rights his phone.

"Alright, good," I say. "I'm going to put myself on mute now."

"No, don't," Cas says quickly. I halt. "I don't mind — I want the background noise. I'll just turn it down."

After a moment Cas goes, "It's weird if you just sit here watching me."

I laugh, quietly. "Okay, I'm gonna work some recipes anyway."

"Mmm," he mumbles. "Vanilla base, peanut butter swirls, no icing but, hear me out, dip the tops in a white chocolate hard shell."

I shake my head. "How bout no?"

His eyes are closed and I give it five, maybe, six seconds before he's out. "That's it," he says dramatically. "I'm taking this brain to your competitors."

"Take your brain to bed."

Calvin Sumner

When I wake, Dres is there.

He doesn't realize I'm awake, his back to me as he washes dishes in the sink. There's music in the background but it's low so I can hear him singing along. The sun's setting, and the kitchens this hazy orange glow. It's a good way to wake up. I feel rested for the first time in a long time.

I lick my lips before putting them together and doing my best street whistle. Dres visibly jumps before he turns around, slinging the dish towel over his shoulder. He leans into his phone. "G'evening sleeping beauty," he says and his tone is way too playful for someone who is in bed with questionable sexual restraint.

"If I'm the beauty, does that make you the brains of this operation? I think this is backwards."

Dres moves, stepping away from the phone. He calls out, "Actually, you're the brains, too." When he returns, he's holding a saucer plate with a cupcake on it. The top looks like it's been painted white. A vanilla hardshell.

"You didn't," I say slowly.

He sets the plate down and then picks up the cupcake, breaking it open down the center. "Peanut butter swirls and all."

If I hadn't already cried my eyes out, I might have started crying again. "I love you a ridiculous amount, you know that?" Dres flushes. As if he needed reminding. "Alright, do me a favor and take a bite but really slow. I need this for my spank bank."

CHAPTER TWO; part two

D resden Gibson

It's May.

And while I like to think that some things do get easier with time, this particular thing, Cas lounging something like ten — twelve feet away, in a pile of blankets and pillows, and me unable to join him, has not. They're my pillows, and my blankets, that I'll take back inside later and sleep on. They'll hold his scent even after he's left. The only thing that lingers longer than his shampoo is the pain of watching him go.

There's nothing standing in my way, nothing that could stop me from opening the screen door and walking out there and joining him. Except that Cas would lose it. We've had this fight enough times now that I can play it in my head like a recording.

And this is better than it's been. He's not stuck on the front stoop, always looking like he's about to leave, even when he's just gotten here. It's actually kind of absurd how long it took us to figure out we could have the same distance with the privacy of the backyard. I got a projector screen so we've been doing movie nights. If not for the fact Cas cuddles with Charlie and Delta and I've got to watch from the doorway like some weird peeping Tom, it's almost like before.

Still, none of this is getting easier. In fact, I think it's just getting harder.

Because he's here, now, and the sun hasn't set yet. He's bathed in a golden light, looking all bronzed and pretty, sprawled across the blankets. His shirt's hiked up a bit, and he's strumming his fingers across the patch of skin between his belly button and the waist band of his sweatpants. His hair's gotten longer, unruly now because he rolled through the grass when he got here with Charlie and Delta. They're lying at his feet, haven't moved since we finished dinner. All of these are reasons I want to be in those blankets with him and not stuck in a chair on the other side of the screen door.

"What're you thinking about?" Cas asks suddenly. He's turned over now onto his stomach to look at me, face propped up on his hand.

"You," I say after a moment.

He perks up at that, smiling. "Good answer."

I say, "True answer."

He turns his head to the side. "What are you thinking about me?"

"What you look like naked," I answer because I know he'll appreciate it.

He laughs loudly. There's a nervousness to the sound. "Better answer." He shifts again, sitting back so he can bring his legs in front of him. "So I actually have some news."

"Bad news?" I ask frowning.

Cas shakes his head quickly. "Good news. Great news, actually. Cases have dropped enough that the ER's back at a working capacity again. Which means that it's no longer all hands on deck. So I actually was able to get PTO approved."

I interrupt him. "For when?"

He laughs again. "Next week would be my last week and then I wouldn't be back at work until June. So I have two covid tests already scheduled and then—."

"You can come home?" Another interruption.

He nods. "Then I can come home."

It feels like every muscle in my body has gone slack, like I've been carrying around tension since the day Cas packed up and left. I lean over in my chair, bracing my arms against my legs. I breathe deeply into my hands that are steepled in front of my mouth.

"You're coming home," I say again, quieter, mostly to myself.

Cas hears me though, and nods. "Yeah, so I'll take my PCR on Sunday and then my rapid test is scheduled for Friday morning so if that's negative I can come home right after."

"It's going to be negative," I tell him, defensive.

"Alright, don't jinx us now. I've managed to avoid this thing for two months. Eventually luck runs out."

"Well now you're just jinxing yourself."

Cas smiles. "In any event, I'm coming home Friday, barring any complications. So clear your schedule, big guy."

I roll my eyes. "Oh, yeah, I'll need to move some things around what with the riveting and booming social life I have."

"Quarantine has made you cynical," he says.

"Quarantine has made me something..."

Has made me miss you in a way that I didn't think was possible. In a way that makes the last five years feel like a primer. Like a lesson in coping from being away from you.

"So then," I say slowly. "What happens when you go back to work?"

I watch his expression, waiting for the face I've seen plenty of times now. The pained, guilty look he gets when he's about to say something I'm not going to like. He never makes the face.

"Well," he responds. "They're going to start giving us rapid tests at the beginning of our shifts. And we'll still be in full PPE and with the numbers on a downward trajectory, I feel good about the risk, or, rather, lack thereof. So if you—."

"I do," I say quickly.

"You didn't even let me—."

"Risk or no risk, I want you to come home permanently."

Cas is pink in the face. "Okay, so I'm coming home permanently, then."

I'm so relieved, I could cry.

Calvin Sumner

The first covid test is the easiest.

I'm unsuspecting, have no idea just how far up my nose they're going to shove this swab. I'm recording the whole thing for Dres, and for posterity's sake, so I play it off like my brain wasn't just tickled. My nurse swirls the swab, pulls it out without ceremony. I lift my finger under my nose to keep myself from sneezing as I give my phone a thumbs up.

The second covid test I'm fully prepared for and already tense before the swab's even been removed from its package. My nurse laughs, can tell this is not my first covid-test rodeo.

Mom gets home sometime after I've been tested. Naturally I left packing up my things to the morning so I'm upstairs finishing that. When I come downstairs, I find her in the living room drinking coffee. She stops me as I'm about to leave. "Heading out?" she calls. While I'm anxious to get back to Dres, I also feel badly about leaving her alone.

She's got time off coming up, too, and is heading down to Florida to check on my grandparents. Not that they need any checking up on. They've been living it up. Even though they insisted they'd follow CDC guidelines, the pandemic south of the Mason-Dixon Line has been the luxury experience.

I step into the room, dropping my two duffle bags at my feet. "Yep, just got the call my rapid's negative, so."

She turns so she can look at me over the back of the sofa. She's holding the mug between her hands, the steam rising in front of her face. "I think it was very," she pauses, "selfless of you. To quarantine away from Dres. A show of real maturity. Not many people could have done that. Or even did. It's why we've been in this hot seat for so long."

"Is it crazy to say this was somehow harder than the last five years away from him? Like this just hurt differently. I don't know."

She smiles softly. "I think it says more about your relationship now. What he means to you. It's not crazy. It's love."

"Okay but does this sound crazy: I think that he may be it for me. I know that life's not a fairytale and obviously this wasn't really some story book romance. But after everything we've been through. I'm just — I'm certain he's the one. Okay, even saying that aloud sounds extremely unrealistic. Or idealistic, I guess. I'm just, wooh — sleep deprivation and all that, just i gnore me."

"Cas," she says in that voice that always precedes a lecture. "Just because it doesn't look like the way our world and media would portray it, doesn't mean it isn't that. Doesn't mean Dres can't be the one or that you can't have a the one. If these last few months have any lessons to offer, it's that you have to be bold enough to live your life. You have to savor every moment of it. If you feel like Dres is the one, then you should let him know so that he can feel it, too."

"That is...actually some of the best advice you've ever given me in your life. Seriously, someone woke up on the sage side of the bed this morning."

She laughs, shaking her head. "Alright, it's been a blast but you're officially evicted."

"You can't evict me when I'm already leaving," I exclaim picking my bags back up. "Okay, well, I'm going to be indisposed for the next three weeks—."

Mom makes a wild noise like I just set a fire in the living room. "Cas, that is too much information!"

"Indisposed because I am officially on vacation and turning my phone off. God, mom, get your head out of the gutter!"

She waves me away. "Get out before you give me an aneurism."

I call Dres when I'm down the street. He picks up on the first ring. Before he can even say hello, I go, "You will not believe this but my test came back positive."

"What?" he practically screams into the phone.

"Yeah, positive for being the most delicious piece of man meat on the market. Crazy, right?"

"Are you — that is not funny, Cas."

"You're right, it's downright hysterical."

"You're not even on the market," he says irritably.

"True, though I may have to put myself on the market if you leave me waiting in our driveway any longer, so."

Dres hangs up on me. Grinning, I get out of my car. When I walk around to the lawn, Dres is there on the stairs staring at me like I could be an aberration. I pause, too, my heart beating fast. It doesn't make sense. This is Dres, after all. I have no reason to be nervous but it suddenly feels like that very first day I stepped foot into Weston's and he walked into the room and my breath left me and never came back. Maybe I'll be waiting all my life for my breath to come back. Maybe it never does. Maybe that's just what it means to be in love.

He moves first, coming down the steps quickly. I run towards him, closing the distance enough so I can fling myself into his arms.

Dres has to take a step back to steady himself but he pulls me tight against his chest, his arms like safety belts across my back. I press my palms down on his shoulders — my shoulders. And then I run them around to his back — my back. I remember this back. Ripped back, beautiful back. Scapula pulled taut as his arms attempt to make a second loop around my torso.

He's got a snake-like hold on me, which makes sense since this is starting to feel like a mating ball occurring on the front lawn.

Dres's head is curled into the side of my neck and he's breathing deeply. His chest expands against mine as he does. The heat of him makes me flushed and I can't really think straight, have to strum my fingers down the back of his neck to ground myself. To remind myself that this is real and really happening. After months of not touching anyone, I'm in Dres's arms and he smells like him.

And like me?

"Are you wearing my cologne?" I ask trying to pull away so I can look at him. Dres hasn't moved at all, nose glued to the junction of my neck that hits my shoulder. "Hello, sir, I'm talking to you. Can you come up for air, please?"

He lifts his head, sliding it up my neck, across the underside of my jaw, a fluid motion that ends unexpectedly with his mouth on mine. He's definitely wearing my cologne and it is so hot, super hot, but not the subject of my focus anymore. Because the kissing? Even hotter.

Dres has tipped me back and his tongue is in my mouth. I cling to his shoulders because it feels like I'm going to fall even though I know, logically, Dres can hold me up. There's more urgency in his kiss than I'm used to. He's kissing me so open and desperate, sliding his tongue over mine like he's trying to deliver a message to my throat. Which might be true because he's making these impatient, whiny sounds and I'm getting the sense that this is simply not close enough and yet I cannot imagine how we could get any closer in this moment. Only I can imagine it and then I do imagine it, and then I remember I don't need to imagine it anymore.

Decidedly, absence makes the heart grow fonder and the dick grow harder.

"Alright, we need to uh," I somehow manage to say despite the urgency as I try to pull away. Dres moves, kissing the side of my face, along my jawline, making me unfocused. "Nope, no, less of that." I reach over, grabbing his chin and holding his face away from mine. He turns his gaze on me, glaring. "We need to move this rodeo into the house because I'm about a second away from whipping my clothes off and making an absolute spectacle on the front lawn."

"So let's make a spectacle, then."

"I— you, you cannot make jokes like that, Dresden Gibson. Not when your boyfriend has tenuous, at best, sexual restraint. Please start moving your feet. I'm serious clothes are coming off in T-minus one."

"What happened to the pillar of restraint?"

"It freaking collapsed when you decided you were going to start wearing my cologne. Seriously, why are you moving so slowly."

I shove Dres ahead of me. My hands are up the back of his teeshirt as he walks across the doorway, already bunching up the fabric. I kick door the closed behind me and he turns, crowding me against it. Before he can lean back in, I reach between us, lifting the hem of his shirt quickly. It's evidently not fast enough for Dres who pulls the fabric the rest of the way before reaching for my own shirt, yanking it over my head.

And then we're kissing again, with the kind of intensity that negates finesse, usurps the need for it. The kind of kiss that knocks at my knees, makes me brace myself against the door so that I don't go down. Dres rakes a hand through my hair, dragging his fingers down towards the curls at the nape of my neck, getting a handful before he yanks on it, tipping my head upwards. I moan into his mouth and he practically swallows the sound as he sucks on my tongue.

I feel my way over his shoulders, along the sharp cut of muscle etched like a horseshoe in the back of his arms, making my way to his pecs. Ah, yes, nipple piercings. My nipple piercings to do with what I see fit. I twirl the barbell in one, pinching the other. Dres makes this sound, sort of high pitched before he shifts his mouth, licking his way over my jaw. I lift my chin so he can get at my neck as I part ways with his chest, moving towards his jeans. Seriously, why is he wearing jeans? I'm commando in sweatpants because I have foresight, know to always come prepared.

I make quick work of the button and zipper but I'm not going to get them off on my own. Dres isn't even paying attention to it, sucking at my neck hard enough to make me dizzy. "Dres, pants — pants, Dres. Take your pants off."

He freaking growls at me like how dare I interrupt. I glare at him. "Excuse me, sir," I say. I don't really know where the 'sir' thing came from but it seems to be working. I'm feeling very sassy today and I jerked off to avoid exactly this so make that make sense. "Sorry but hickeys are like a lazy post-coital thing. There's allll the time in the world for hickeys but I'm currently in a sex fog that isn't going to be cured by some necking."

"A sex fog?" Dres repeats, his tone amused as he raises an eyebrow at me. Evidently, necking is the cure-all for him. He seems perfectly at ease for someone who was trying to swallow my whole face seconds ago on the front lawn. Explain this sorcery.

"Are you fucking me or not because I'm about to go put myself on the market. The black market. With a caption that reads my very hot boyfriend is treating me like a ninth grade hook up and I'm in need of — oh. Yes, that is, yep, that." Dres has stepped out of his jeans and shucked my sweatpants in the span of my little spiel. He's got his hand on me, jerking me slowly even though I'm already at full attention, leaking into his fist. He's dipped his head back in, planting wet kisses down my throat. They match the painstaking pace he's set with his hands.

"Listen, I'm feeling very much like a hair trigger right now, like it would actually be embarrassing how much I am not gonna last here if I had the capacity to be embarrassed, which I do not because I'm using every ounce of energy here to not die. And so while I would love to draw this out and get oh-so-reacquainted with that body of yours I'm gonna need us to skip ahead to the end credits scene. Because if the first thing I do after quarantining from you for months is cum into your fist, I'm not gonna lie I'm gonna be a little pissed about it. Dres, are you even freaking listening to me right now? Stop doing that."

Dres freezes, pulling away completely. I repress a whine. I wanted him to stop but also did not want him to stop at all. He's looking at me now and I have no idea what's happening until he says, "I cannot believe how much I've missed these monologues of yours."

"I mean, that was more like a lament, but oh—."

Dres shuts me up as he slides an arm around my waist and lifts me easily, like I weigh nothing. I don't weigh nothing, but I have lost weight. Long hours, stress, lack of sleep, and the fact I wear seventeen pounds of PPE that's more effort to take off than food is worth evidently. Still, the fact Dres can lift me like this is a testimony to his strength. It's also super dup er hot.

I expect him to walk us into the living room, or my favorite room to deface, the kitchen, but he doesn't, stepping forward instead, so I'm braced against the door.

"Oh," I repeat tightening my legs around the backs of his thighs. I hook my heels for leverage and grip his shoulders. "I can get down with this. Also, I'm very much prepped and ready to go."

He laughs and the sound vibrates against my sternum where his head is pressed. "I figured as much."

And that's about all the warning I get before Dres gets his dick in me. And not in a drawn out, inch by inch sort of way. In an instance, he's buried deep. We stopped using condoms when I moved in. We both got tested, talked extensively about the implications of not using protection. There's a lot of trust you're putting in someone when you take away that barrier. I hadn't understood that the first time we'd done it, but I did now. And it was good, knowing that we were both on the same page.

"Loosen your legs a bit," he says. His voice is tight. I wonder if I'm hurting h im.

"We could totally take it to the floor," I say but I don't exactly mean it. It feels like I'm being fucked in space, like I'm levitating, and it's the kind of intensity that could make me weep. Even though Dres is hardly moving. It's the press of him inside me, how he's buried to the base and panting against my chest. Gravity is working in our favor.

I rest my chin on his head, which smells like me, also. I definitely took my shampoo when I left so Dres had to have ordered his own. That's enough to punch an orgasm out of me. I could probably get an award for that. World's Fastest Orgasm Brought On by Scent.

"Cas," Dres says and I try to look at him but it's hard at this angle. "Let your legs go."

I know my expression is skeptical. "Is that a good idea?"

"I've got you," he says and I believe him, trust him, so I unhook the heels of my feet from the insides of his knees, letting them sort of dangle.

He does have me, all of me really. I'm suspended against the door. Dres shifts me downwards, hiking my legs up between us so my knees are pressed against his chest. The suddenness of it, the angle and movement, jolts me. I pinch my eyes closed, taking an uneasy breath. It's good, it's really good, everyone should be fucked against a door once or maybe ten times in their life. I think we'll just have to work this into our weekly rotation.

I get control of myself. Mindful breathing is helping. I open my eyes, meeting Dres's gaze. It's intensely focused, his eyebrows pulled taut. I'd laugh if my body wasn't contorted like a pretzel.

And, anyway, the concept of laughing dissipates pretty quickly. Somehow, despite the gravity-defying physics of it, Dres is fucking up into me. Short thrusts that deliver a bolt of pleasure each time that makes the blood simmer where his hands are holding me. All the blood in my body is clearly trying to move to my dick, which couldn't get any harder if I delivered a shot of viagra right into it.

It's over way too soon. It was always going to be way too soon, though.

I think I'd like to stay here, against this door, with Dres, forever. It's all very crazy when I think about it. About what he means to me, has always meant to me. I was holding out hope, even when I'd stopped writing, even when I hated him. There was never going to be anyone else, but Dres, for me. Not because of destiny, not because we were fated and this is true love. But because I chose him, I decided on him. He's who I want to spend the rest of my life with and I should probably tell him that, but not right now. I don't think I can make coherent sentences as it stands.

I press my palms to his face, one on each cheek. He's rosy and his cheeks are hot. But he's beautiful and I am having a hard time digesting all of this. That I'm back home, here, with him. And then because my brain is stupid, I start thinking about all the people who have died, of the people I had to FaceTime and tell them that their partner was dying, and they should say goodbye. I am so lucky, I think, that it wasn't me. That it wasn't us.

"Don't cry," Dres says suddenly which is like exactly what you don't say.

"I'm not," I say which is like exactly what you do say when...

"You are."

So I just drop my head and leave it there on his shoulder. He has to be getting tired holding me up but I can't move just yet. I'm still waiting for the blood to drain from my dick and return to my extremities.

"What's wrong?" he asks quietly.

"Nothing," I mumble into his arm. "Nothing's wrong. Everything's right."

"Then why are you crying?"

"Because I'm so — I'm just so...grateful. I feel very grateful for this little life."

"This little life," he repeats back after a moment. He's always doing that. Repeating me.

"So I know it's like not even noon but would it really be absurd if we went to bed right now?"

I want to lay with you is what I don't say.

I want to curl up against you and use your heat as a blanket.

I want to be with you in my dreams, too.

Dres doesn't answer but he starts walking, takes me upstairs just like that, clinging to his chest. When we get upstairs, he walks to his bed and dumps me there before disappearing into the bathroom. I land with a bounce. Not his bed, I realize. Our bed. My bed again. A much nicer bed than the one at my mom's. Smells deliciously of Dres.

"Oh, sweet bed, how I missed thee," I say as I throw my arms and legs out like a starfish.

"Don't move," Dres calls before he returns to the room carrying a washcloth.

"You and your sheets," I mock quietly. God forbid a body fluid touch them. Not when they're a million thread count Egyptian cotton.

He kneels above me, cleaning me in that weird meticulous way he has a tendency to do. "Can I move now?" I ask when he's finished. He gives me an unamused look. I throw a leg out, wrapping it around his hip as best I can so I can push him down and roll onto him.

"What is this?" he asks now very much amused. I burrow my head into his neck, nipping at the thick muscle that makes up his traps. "I thought coming to bed meant you wanted to sleep?"

"I do but I also need to re-familiarize myself with this foreign body in bed with me."

"What am I a UFO?"

"Among other things," I mumble into his suprasternal notch. I sprawl out against his body, pressing my arms against his and my legs against his so we're stacked like pancakes.

"Other things?" he asks quietly.

"You're the love of my life first," I say. "UFO second, meh-communicator third."

"My communication skills are a bit more than meh, I think," he responds but his voice is off.

"Are they, though?" I ask, lifting my head so I can look up at him. He has to tuck his chin down to make eye contact. He brings his hand up to my face. I place my hand over his.

"Love of your life?"

"This life, the next life, the one before. All of them, I think."

Dres is quiet for a moment. I rest my chin on his chest so I'm still looking at him but not straining. He's looking at me. Finally, he says, "You're being very candid today."

I bite my lip, nodding my head slightly. I say, "If you love someone, you should let them know so they can feel it, too."

"I can feel it."

I let us have this moment.

But because I'm also unapologetically me, I break the silence with, "Well that actually may be my dick that you're feeling."

Dres jabs me in the side. "You're ridiculous," he says but he's laughing.

"But you lurveee it," I croon as I roll off of him. I really did want to go to sleep. There's going to be a round two, probably three, possibly four today. Gonna need the sleep to replenish my energy.

I swing my leg back over his hips and an arm, too, because decidedly he can't move or leave until I've had my fill of touching him, which may take a week or so.

Dres isn't complaining, lifting his arm up in the air so I can tuck myself up against his side. I'm half-asleep when Dres says, "I just want you to know."

Drowsy, getting drowsier by the second, I repeat back, "You just want me to know."

"I fully intend to marry you."

"Not if I marry you first."

"Oh, is it a competition now?"

"Yeah, I'll race you to the alter."

"I'm faster than you."

"That may be true, but I play dirty. I'll trip you."

"You'll probably trip yourself."

"Funny guy."

"I'm serious though."

"About which part?"

"The first part."

"Yeah," I say after a moment. "I'm serious about that, too."

CHAPTER THREE; part one

February 2020 (pre-covid)

Dresden Gibson

"Let's go away one weekend," I say to Cas over dinner. He looks tired, and he's doing paperwork on his laptop as he spoons soup into his mouth. It's February, and it's frigid, so soup. Cas doesn't always work at dinner — actually he really never works at dinner — but he brings work home a lot. He says he's got to do it either way, and he can stay at work or have eye candy while he does his charts. I'm eye candy, evidently.

He's rubbing at his eyebrow, which means he's about to get a headache. "Cas," I say, and he looks over at me like he's just now hearing me. "What do you think? A weekend away?"

"A weekend away where and when?" he asks as he pushes his glasses up his nose.

"In two weeks," I answer evenly. "I know a place."

"You know a place? That sounds like a ditch the body place."

"You got me," I deadpan. "Drag you to the middle of nowhere and bury you where nobody would ever think to look."

"Have you learned nothing from our How to Get Away with Murder binge? You need to burn my body. No body, no crime." He rolls his eyes over-dramatically and then glances back at his computer. "It has been so freaking busy in the ER lately. I am in desperate need of a break. I will literally put my PTO in now. What days?"

I aim for casual when I answer, "Thirteenth to the sixteenth."

"Thirteenth to theeee," Cas repeats as he clicks at his computer. "Wait a minute. Wait a gosh darn minute. That is Valentine's Day weekend."

"Oh, is that Valentine's Day? I had no idea," I say.

Cas pins me down with a questioning stare. "What are you planning?"

I shrug noncommittally. "I'm not planning anything."

I've started walking away and flinch at the screech of the bar stool grating against the floor as Cas hops to his feet. He runs over, tackling me from behind so that I nearly go down. "What is this?" I call out, leveraging myself with a hand on the back of the couch.

Cas has his arms flung over my shoulders and the weight of him is on my back. "Tell me what you're planning," he demands.

"I'm not planning anything," I respond calmly. "You're going to bring us down if you don't stop squirming."

He reaches across my chest and pinches my nipple through my shirt. He's careful because of the piercing but it still hurts. "Ow, Cas, what are you doing?"

"Tell me," he whines. "This is so unfair. I literally never see your surprises coming."

"That's the point of a surprise, isn't it?" I ask.

"Tell me what the surprise is," he repeats.

"There isn't a surprise. I just want to go away with you."

"To an undisclosed location. On Valentine's Day. Right."

"Well, yeah it sounds suspect when you say it like that — can you please stop pinching my nipple now?"

Cas laughs into my ear but doesn't stop. "Why? Is it turning you on?"

"You got me," I muse taking a few steps forward before I turn and dump Cas onto the couch. I slump beside him and he wastes no time sliding his head into my lap, looking up at me.

"You're always doing things," he says pitifully. "I need to get a PI."

I grin. "So unnecessary."

"So where are we going then?"

"New Hampshire."

"What's in New Hampshire?"

"You'll see."

"I hate this game."

"S'not a game."

"One day," he says wistfully.

"One day what exactly?"

"I'm going to surprise attack you back. A surprise so huge and you're not even gonna see it coming."

"I'll believe it when I see it," I say quietly, running my hand through his hair. Cas's eyes start to close like I'm lulling him to sleep with my ministrations.

"You will," he mumbles. "And when you see it you'll be so shocked. You'll say how in the world did he get this one past me..."

"You're falling asleep," I say with a soft laugh.

"Quick nap," Cas responds and he's out, just like that.

Cas is asleep in the passenger seat. I'm not entirely sure he ever actually woke up, more like sleep-crawled his way downstairs and out to the car at seven a.m. I wanted to get an early start since we have about a five hour drive ahead of us, not factoring in traffic.

He wakes when we're just getting into Massachusetts, coming to with a jolt so that he springs forward in his seat, looking around bewildered like I've kidnapped him. "Mmmm," he says stretching. He twists next and his back cracks. "Where are we?"

"I think we're about to pass through Auburn. In Massachusetts."

He frowns. "How much longer do we have?"

I tap my phone screen that's clipped to a stand in my vent. Cas looks. "Two more hours?" he wails. "How are there still two more hours? I thought I slept for like six."

I manage to fight back a grin long enough to say coolly, "So you're obviously not a road tripper."

He turns to glare at me. "So you're obviously not a road tripper," he mocks and I can't fight back my laughter. He frowns, shoulders sagging low. "Long car rides kill me."

It's not shocking news. Asking Cas to sit still in a confined space for more than hour? A feat in itself. He's a toddler like that, always has been I think.

"Five hours is not a long car ride. If we drove to Florida, it'd be sixteen hours. That's a long car ride."

"Why in the world would we ever drive to Florida when we could fly? Tell me you're not thinking of driving to Florida next because I will seriously book a flight and meet you there."

I shake my head. We apparently woke up on the over dramatic side of the bed today. "There's something nice about the open road. You can sight see, stop at landmarks. Get one of those Weird Roadside Attractions pamphlet-things from the gas station."

"I'm sorry, one of those what? Why does it feel like you've thought about this extensively."

"I just like road tripping. Maybe I'll buy an RV."

"And put it where, exactly? You'd also have to take time off to actually use it, you realize? Actually hand over the Weston reigns to Dolores and Charles."

I grimace. "I think I'm more apt to put Tasha in charge if I'm being honest."

Cas makes a face. It's not a jealous face, more like surprised. "You trust her like that? How long has she even been working with you?"

"It'll be three years in May. When I hired her she'd just had a daughter and was trying to finish college. She needed help so..." I don't know what I'm trying to say exactly.

"So naturally you helped her," Cas says but it's not an accusation. He says it like it's just a fact. Like that's who I am. Maybe it is. "Well, I really like her. She's spunky."

I shake my head. "More like intrusive, opinionated, and bossy."

Cas makes eyes at me. "Wow, you really do have a type."

"Ha ha."

Cas sits back, pulling his legs up onto the seat. "So what's Rumi's deal?"

"Teen angst, mainly."

He laughs. "I know it well."

I laugh too. That he does. "I don't know. I guess she's constantly looking for validation in relationships. Which isn't all that unusual for her age. But she romanticizes everything. So it's like every other week some poor soul's letting her down or failing to live up to the idea of them she's created in her head."

"Huh. Is she straight?"

"You seriously have no gaydar."

He throws his hands up. "Whatever. Jack is freaking effeminate as hell and you two flirt with each other all the time. An honest mistake."

"Jack flirts with anything that has ears and can understand him. Flirting is the natural tone of his voice. Anyway, I think Rumi's bi. She says she falls on the Kinsey scale. So whatever that means."

"I, too, fall on the Kinsey scale."

"Yeah? And where do you fall exactly?"

He turns and grins at me. "On you, duh."

I roll my eyes but am fighting back a grin as I do. "Hanging onto that one for a while?"

"Have literally been racking my brain for weeks on how I could casually work Kinsey scale into conversation."

"You're ridiculous."

"Mmm," he agrees. "Okay, how much time has passed? We had to have at least shaved off an hour — are you freaking kidding me, how do we still have two hours to go? The time hasn't changed. Are we even moving? I'm going to lose it, Dres. That's it, I'm losing it. I'm lost." He throws himself dramatically against the dash.

"Will you relax? Look, go in the side pocket of my bag. The big pocket. There's something in there for you."

He turns excitedly, pulling my bag into his lap. "Is it food?" he asks as he unzips the pocket.

"No, why? Are you hungry?"

"Because it's ninety-nine percent of the time always food with you. Oh shit! You remembered. I was going to pick this up eventually." Cas holds out the book in his hands, admiring the cover. Suddenly, he mutters, "You're out here listening to me and shit." He says it accusatorially, making it feel less like a compliment and more of a problem.

"Why do you sound mad?"

"I don't know, Dres, maybe I wanted to buy this for myself."

"Wait, are you actually mad?"

"I don't know, Dres. I don't know. Stop asking me questions." I frown at the road in front of me, gripping the wheel tighter then I need to. I can feel the tension in my shoulders, making my elbows lock and knuckles go white. If Cas is mad about the book, this whole weekend's going to be a bust.

"Fuck, I love you," he says breaching the silence. The words leave him like he's releasing some frustration.

My elbows unlock. I drop one hand onto my knee. I aim for casual when I say, "So...you're not mad then?"

He laughs quietly. "No, I'm not mad. Of course I'm not mad. I'm just like — why are you so good to me?"

"Why can't I just be good to you?"

Cas turns then, shoving my bag onto onto the floor before he unbuckles his seatbelt and slides over. Before I can register what's happening, he's reaching into my lap and undoing my pants. I glance down at his hand and then back up at the road. "What are you doing?" I blurt. My heart rate picks up, which is just reactionary to Cas at this point.

"Being good to you back."

We shave another hour off the drive, stopping once in Boston to grab something to eat at this local chain, Life Alive. It's a vegan spot and Cas grumbles about it — "you would manage to locate some hoity-toity health restaurant" but then rectifies shortly after "I would consider converting for this avocado mousse." We stop again in Lowell to stretch and use a rest room. The book was the best decision I made, a selfish one really, because it's kept Cas mostly quiet.

Mostly.

Every so often he has some sudden outburst. Like now, breaking the silence with: "Oh my freaking god!"

"What?" I practically scream back jolted from my dazing.

Cas waves a hand at me like I'm the one who's had some sudden outburst and should be more mindful. "Nothing, nothing, the plot is thickening that's all."

Silence ensues only to be broken again by Cas. "I swear to fucking god. Cops are so dirty. I'm disgusted. I can't keep reading." He tosses the book dramatically onto the seat.

I glance at it and up at him before turning my gaze back to the road. I'm counting quietly, get to six before he picks it back up. "I'm gonna lose it," he mumbles, but he lifts his legs onto the seat and starts reading again. I need to remember to get another book for the ride home. In retrospect, I don't know why I thought he could handle this drive without one.

It's nearing three when we finally get into Wolfeboro. The temperature dropped dramatically when we crossed the edge of Massachusetts into New Hampshire and there's snow everywhere, flakes falling as we drive through town. The sky's a stony white and it's already dark out.

Cas hasn't really noticed, turning pages in his book like his life depends on it. The GPS directs me down a narrow icy road, and I sort of recognize the winding tree-lined path. I'd only been up here twice before, once when I was looking at real estate two winters ago, and then again last summer when I'd closed on the place.

It's pretty up here, the trees bare and covered in frost and snow. The Wolfeboro Bay's, to my left, is frozen over and untouched.

"Hey," I say. Cas lowers his book, looking at me over the edge of it. "What are the odds I get you to close your eyes and cooperate without throwing a fit?"

He slams the book down completely. "I knew it! I freaking knew it. You planned something. You're literally always doing something."

I answer myself. "Odds are slim to none apparently."

"Why does everything have to be all huge surprises with you? One day I'm just gonna have a heart attack. A massive cardiac episode and you're going to have to tell all our friends yeah, you know, I surprised him to death."

While Cas laments, I turn into the driveway. The house is hidden behind trees, and we have to drive up to it. There's a light coat of snow on the ground that is starting to cover tire tracks. I hired someone to maintain the house while I was away and they came earlier to see through some tasks to open it.

I point up at the windshield after I put the truck in park. "So I bought a lake house. Surprise."

Cas's face squishes together. He glances back and forth between me and the house several times. "You bought a lake house?"

"Yes."

"That's your second home?"

"Well," I say pausing. "Our second home now."

Cas looks at me and I don't know what his expression means exactly. "Well let's see the inside then," he says finally, hopping out before I can make sense of what's just happened. Cas darts up the walkway to the door but I'm slow to follow, breathing in the crisp air as I step out of the car. We're nestled in a patch of woods, right on the water, and it smells like pine and earth. The smell alone could convince me to move out here, even though it's remote, at least a twenty minute drive into town where there's limited shopping options.

"Why are you so slow?" Cas screams at me as I walk up. "It's not exactly warm."

"Well where's your coat?" I ask as I type the code into the keypad. Cas repeats my question mockingly. I push the front door open and let him i n.

"Oh," he says and it's not likely an exclamation of awe. I have to bite back a laugh. He walks in, stepping through the foyer towards the living room. It's an open floor plan, a preference of mine, with the kitchen to our left and an open-tread staircase directly in the entryway. There are floor to ceiling windows to our right that looks out onto the water.

"It's very, uhm, modern. Simplistic."

I follow behind him as he walks through what would be the living room. At the moment, its empty save for the brick fireplace cutting the windows into two sections, and a tv mounted above it. There aren't even seats.

I try to keep my tone level when I say, "You like it, right? I wanted something minimalistic."

"More like the bare minimalistic," Cas remarks quietly enough I don't think he wants me to hear it. I watch as he spins around, peering past me towards the kitchen. "Well, the kitchen looks really nice. I don't really understand this living concept, though. Do you stand while you watch tv? Is that supposed to be a health-conscious thing? Your apple watch will certainly love you."

"Come see the upstairs," I say taking his hand and dragging him towards the stairs.

"Do you have something against art?" he asks as we go up. "Like I know you couldn't because you're covered in it. So I am confused."

It's taking everything in me not to laugh. "There's something about the bare walls. Especially because the paints so nice."

"The walls are painted white, Dres," Cas says sounding like he thinks I'm crazy. I drag him into one of the guest bedrooms.

"What do you think?" I ask.

Cas raises an eyebrow. "Is this a joke?"

"These walls are actually Swiss coffee. Downstairs was promenade. You see the difference, right?"

Cas raises both his eyebrows. "Literally white walls. These are white, downstairs is white. Promenade? Swiss coffee? They're both the freaking same."

I frown forcibly because it's the only thing preventing me from grinning. "You don't like it."

"No," Cas says quickly throwing a hand out like he can physically stop the idea. "I do. It's a really nice place. I'm just trying to understand why its empty? Like where are we sleeping? On the floor? Ohhhh, is this like a camping thing? Did you pack like a tent and sleeping bags? Is that the gag?"

I shake my head. "No, no that's not the gag."

Cas frowns, staring at me hard, working to figure it out. I step around him, pressing myself against his back. He makes a squeaky sound that comes out with a laugh. "What are you doing?"

It's a cute thing that I can still make him nervous. I reach up and cover his eyes. Cas grabs at my wrists but doesn't move my hands away. "What color should we paint the walls of our guest room?" I ask.

I feel his eyebrows move under my fingers. "What?"

"Think about our guest room. What color walls does it have?"

"This again," he grumbles. "Okay, fine, I'll play ball. Green."

"You want to paint this room green?"

"Well, I don't know, what do you want?"

"Cas," I say dropping my chin onto his shoulder so I'm talking into his ear. "I want you to decorate our house."

"Come again," he says moving my hands away from his eyes so he can turn around to look at me. "You want me to decorate?" I nod. "The whole house?" I nod again. "Which is why it's empty."

"Which is why it's empty," I repeat back. "Except for the master bedroom because we need somewhere to sleep for the weekend."

He nods thoughtfully. "I like light grey for the walls. Maybe a subtle blue."

"Whatever you want."

Cas drapes his arms over my shoulders, leaning into me. "Whatever I want? I like the sound of that."

"Within reason," I add because I know that tone of voice.

"Sex swing and a stripper pole."

"You can have one," I say and before I've even gotten the full sentence out Cas is beaming at me with all his teeth.

"Ha! I only wanted the sex swing anyway." I roll my eyes. Cas goes, "So I'm decorating a whole house."

"It'll be good practice."

Cas stares at me, but doesn't comment on what I'm insinuating. Then he says, "Oh, wait, does that mean I'm decorating the kitchen, then, if I'm decorating the whole house?"

I try to interrupt him but he keeps going.

"Because I'm feeling one of those double sinks with a long gooseneck kind of faucet but it doesn't detach — oh my god the face you are making right now."

Cas laughs at me and I say quickly, "So one caveat to decorating the whole house."

He pokes my stomach. "What you don't love the idea of an electric stove and laminate countertops?"

"That's an actual nightmare."

"I know, it's what you whisper in your sleep. No, no, not the formica. Anything but the formica!"

"I don't talk in my sleep."

"Oh, you really do. You alternate between that and describing all the dirty, vile, delicious things you want to do to me."

"Uh-huh, right, this is starting to sound more like your dreams."

"Well in my dreams you're doing it, not describing it, to me." Cas slides his hands down to the neckline of my sweater, tugging on the fabric as he says, "So the bedrooms furnished right?"

I cup his hands with mine, mostly to keep him from moving them any-where else. "It is. I need to run into town though and get groceries but you can stay here and take a nap."

"I wasn't asking about the bedroom so I could nap," Cas mumbles.

I laugh. "Oh, I'm aware. I need to get groceries otherwise we're going to starve. There's nothing here."

"Okay, okay." He takes his hands away to hold them up in the air. "I'll go with you."

I say as I lead the way back downstairs, "We can go in the hot tub later."

"Hot tub? Now you're speaking my language."

CHAPTER THREE; part two

February 2020 (pre-covid)

Calvin Sumner

"It's freaking freezing out here," I scream, wrapping my arms around myself as I run across the back deck. Dres is moving leisurely, of course, at the speed he seems to prefer to move at, particularly in ten degree weather.

My teeth are chattering when I tell him to hurry up, bouncing on my feet like that may increase blood flow enough to warm me up even a fraction of a degree. It doesn't.

Dres runs up behind me and picks me up unexpectedly, throwing me over his shoulder like I weigh nothing. I scream his name and can feel his shoulders shaking under my hips as he laughs, moving swiftly down the stone pathway towards the hot tub.

He walks us into the center of the tub before he sets me down. I let out a sound of satisfaction when my feet submerge into the hot water, turning towards the nearest wall and crouching down against it without hesitation.

I sink low enough that the water grazes my chin. Dres remains standing, looking mildly uncomfortable.

"Is it supposed to be this hot? It feels too hot."

"No, it's perfect. This feels so good. Come on, sit down." I slap the water. "You just need to get used to it."

Dres eventually sits down across from me, leaning back against the side. Most of his chest is above the water and his arms are sprawled across the back. He looks posed, like he's sitting for someone who's going to paint his portrait, even though he's clearly not trying. His eyes are closed and his heads tipped back. He could be sleeping.

I kind of want to put my mouth on him but I've been trying to exercise restraint.

Okay, so I just decided in this moment I'm going to exercise restraint. Because sex in a hot tub doesn't really have that much appeal to me.

The silence must tip Dres off because he opens his eyes and tilts his head to look at me. "What?" he asks, amusement in his tone.

"Nothing, you're just breathtaking, is all," I say in the most casual of tones.

Dres flushes. "Stop it."

"I'm just saying."

"Don't just say," he grumbles.

"You need to learn how to take a compliment. Here, try it with me. Thank you, baby, that's so nice of you to say."

Dres is like really flushing. I want to chalk it up to the hot water, but I'm certain it's my words. Dres doesn't do well with compliments but he's going to have to work through that because there's lots of them in his future. I kind of think despite how poorly he takes them, that he needs them. Maybe even likes hearing nice things about himself.

He's flustered now, though, as he grasps for a response. "I'm not calling you that."

"Fine," I say with an exaggerated eye roll, even though I'd really be on board with baby as a pet-name. Especially if it's coming out of Dres's mouth. Super hot. "Thank you, darling, that's so nice of you to say."

"No."

"Thank you, sweetheart, that's so nice of you to say."

Dres pushes away from the wall and wades over to me, climbing into my lap like this segue is a very natural progression. But Dres in my lap is not something I'll ever be equipped to handle, always feels like the best kind of surprise.

He sits down and I wrap my arms around his lower back loosely. "Thank you," he says, voice low, as he dips his head and kisses at the underside of my jaw. "Sweetheart," he kisses at the other side of my jaw, "darling," and then the center of my throat before he licks his way up over my chin.

"Baby," he says into my mouth as he kisses me. I move my hands, reaching up to cup his face and hold him there. He parts too soon and I've all but forgotten about my call for restraint. So I get a chlorine-cleaning, big whoop. I'll cross the medical ramifications of that bridge later.

"That's so nice of you to say," he says mouth hovering over mine. I can feel his lips moving with each word.

I make a disgruntled sound. "You're a tease."

He bats his lashes. "Oh, whatever do you mean."

"You know exactly what I mean —" I break off with a groan. "I swear to god, Dres if you don't stop rocking in my lap."

"You're gonna what?" he asks nudging my nose with his. "Fuck me?"

It's so unexpected that I jerk my head backwards, and Dres looks at me, surprised, and I'm definitely looking at him surprised. I open my mouth to speak but don't know what to say at first, giving it a moment before I go, "I didn't think you'd want to again."

Dres's eyebrows pull together, confused. "Why?"

"I don't know. I wasn't very good the first time."

Dres glares at me like I've personally offended him. Like I've just said he wasn't that good. "Says who?"

Okay, admittedly, I'd just sort of assumed it wasn't that great for Dres. It was freaking fantastic for me. I'd be chasing that feeling for the rest of my l ife.

"Cas," Dres says and he nudges at my forehead with his so I'll look up. "It was good for me." He waits for my reaction or response and when I don't give one, he goes, "It was good for me. Okay?"

"Okay," I repeat back if only to get him to stop looking at me like that.

"I would do it again," he says finally. "I would like to if you want to."

"I don't know," I answer quickly. "I just feel like I wasn't — and I don't really know how — and it's just, it was really intense and it's a lot, you know, overwhelming and I'm nervous. I'm nervous to—"

"Cas," Dres says, cutting me off. "It's just us. It's not like there's an audi- ence."

"Just us, like you aren't you."

"What does that even mean?"

"It means—" I sigh heavily, a nauseating combination of frustrated and embarrassed. "It is intimidating enough to be doing something I'm not used to doing and then to be doing that thing with you..."

Dres frowns. "So did you not want to do it the first time?"

"No," I say quickly. "No, I did. I do. I just — I want to impress you. That's it, that's all it is. I want to impress you."

"Sex is the one place you don't have to worry about impressing me." He says it so seriously that I suddenly feel like I've built up all this anxiety around topping for absolutely no reason at all. "I like our sex life, Cas. It's not unsatisfying in the least. But it's also not the reason I'm with you at all. I don't need some stallion in the sheets. What I like about sex is that I'm having it with you."

"Oh," I say quietly. "Okay." I drop my head on his shoulder, whispering into his neck, "You make me nervous and I keep expecting that feeling to go away but it doesn't."

He caresses the back of my head. "Maybe feeling a little nervous is a good thing. Or maybe it's not nerves at all that you're feeling."

I know exactly what I'm feeling, though. This sense of dread coupled with the embarrassing response to give him everything I am and everything I have to give. I'm not really trying to impress Dres, that's not what makes me nervous. I'm trying to convey a bigger message than I know words for, something that says you can harve every inch of me, it's all yours. I'm nervous because it constantly feels like I have something to lose.

So maybe I'm just crazy. Maybe that's all you can be when you love someone so vigorously.

"Come on," I say.

"Where are we going?"

"Where do you think? To the bedroom for a Cas tops Dres part two. Giving it the ol' college try."

"We really don't have to, if you really don't want to."

"I really do want to but I really can't overthink it or I'm going to vomit on you."

"That's one way to foreplay."

So it goes if at first you don't succeed, try again.

Because apparently you will succeed.

Topping 0 Cas 1

The sex endorphins haven't worn off yet and I'm feeling too good. Good enough that it doesn't even bother me that topping leaves me way sweatier and I could benefit from a shower right about now. I'm not going to shower, though, because Dres is wrapped around me, head resting on my chest and his arms tucked under mine, linking across my back. One could say I was big spooning and they would be close to accurate. And I never big spoon. I'm just going to enjoy this in all my sweaty glory.

I run my hand along his shoulder blades and then up over the curve of his arm. I remember the feel of it, how the flesh rises slightly and is softer than the rest of him. Feels delicate, feels like a thin sheet of skin draped over a memory.

"What are the odds this place is haunted?" I whisper.

Dres grumbles and sounds half-asleep when he answers, "It's not haunted."

"But like what are the odds it is?" I ask.

"There are no odds," he says.

"But those are odds. The odds are zero, then."

"It's not haunted, Cas."

"I think I heard something."

"You didn't. Go to sleep."

I close my eyes but I can't quell the weird panicky feeling in my stomach and that spot on Dres's shoulder feels hotter than the rest of him, like it's burning to warn me. I don't really believe in ghosts. And I don't actually think this place is haunted. No, what I really think is this place just isn't secure.

"Do you think someone could break into here?"

Dres unravels himself, shifting up the bed so his head's on the same pillow as me. "What's going on?"

"I didn't lock any doors, did you lock the doors?"

Dres gives a curt nod. "Yes, I locked the doors. Do you want me to double-check?"

"I believe you," I say after a moment and then, "Why don't we have an alarm on this place?"

"We can get one," he answers.

"But what if someone breaks in tonight?"

Dres gives me a weird look. "No ones breaking in tonight. No ones breaking in any night."

"But I heard something."

"You didn't hear anything."

And then I hear something again. Louder. Definitive. My eyes are wide as I stare at Dres, who seems perfectly unfazed.

He huffs. "I'll go check."

"No!" I reach out to stop him as he sits up. "You've already been shot twice. Statistically, it's unlikely you'd survive a third."

"Wait, what does that even—?"

I interrupt him, continuing, "It could be another psycho stalker who wants to shoot the gay vet. Yeah, no, I'll go check."

I push the covers off of me as Dres goes, "Well I'm going with you.'

Because the house is not furnished in the slightest, there's nothing to bring with me as a weapon. I grab Dres's boot by the door as we step out into the hallway. Dres is in front of me, leading the way like there is nothing to fear as I creep behind him.

"You're walking too loudly," I whisper.

Dres glances over his shoulder so I can see just how unamused he is. It's not like I imagined the noise. We get to the stairwell and it's dark downstairs, save for light streaming through the front door. Which means someone was outside our front door because the outdoor lights are on a sensor. I'm definitely not imagining things. There's someone in the house.

We walk downstairs and I'm quiet but Dres is not. He's strolling like there isn't any imminent danger. As we round the corner into the living room, I get in front of him just in case someone's waiting for us with a shotgun.

"What are you doing?" he asks his tone confused and amused. "And why do you have my shoe? What are you going to do with that?"

"Throw it at the person who's clearly broken into our house," I respond.

"There's no one down here," he says as he flips on the light switch. It's way too bright for this time of night and I have to squint before I get used to it. There's a loud crash outside, on the deck, and I visibly jump.

"I'll go check it out," he says calmly.

I grab his arm, stopping him from continuing towards the back door. "Maybe we should just call the police. They can do a walk around."

"Cas," he says softly. "There's no one out there."

"You don't know that," I snap, frustrated by how lightly he's taking this.

The night he came into my ER with a gunshot wound, he'd told the police that the guy who shot him told him to beg. Of course he didn't. I honestly wouldn't have expected him to, though, I would've hoped some self preservation would've kicked in. No, instead, Dres said something utterly ridiculous, something like 'we wear the same uniform,' to a guy who hated the fact a gay man had served in the military.

Dres takes risks, puts his life at risk, and I'm simply not okay with that.

"Alright, come on, we'll check it out together." Dres pulls me towards him, holding my hand as he leads the way. He opens the back door and we step out onto the porch. My adrenaline isn't so that I don't immediately feel frozen to the bone. I'm barefoot and only wearing the boxers I'd pulled on before we'd come downstairs. Goosebumps rise on my arms and legs. It's so cold my nose instantly starts running.

I dart my gaze along the tree-line near the lake. If someone was here, they were probably spooked by the lights and would've retreated into the darkness. They've probably got a sniper trained on us right now. We should run back inside before the both of us get shot.

Admittedly, I know I'm sort of running with these thoughts now. I'm about to apologize to Dres for dragging us down here when his hand squeezes mine. "Cas," he says, tone very calm. Like forcibly so. "I need you not to scream."

My stomach drops into my ass. I was right. There's a freaking sniper in the woods. I glance down at my chest to see if the little red dot is floating on my skin. It's not

I turn to look where Dres is looking and meet two white orbs in the darkness. The bears a short distance away, at the end of our deck, hovering in the darkness. It's big but I don't know by what standards. I've never seen a bear in its natural habitat before.

"Oh," I say as Dres takes a step back and then tugs me into his chest. His arm crosses over my chest as he practically drags me backwards into the house. My legs are so cold they've locked up and have stopped working. That may also be a fear response.

I watch him shut the door softly and then turn the lock.

"So do we call animal control? Should we make a run for the car? Like what's the protocol for this. I have never seen a bear outside of the zoo before."

Dres chuckles. "No, it'll be gone by the morning. I'm surprised it was even out and not hibernating. But it's not going to bother us." Dres puts his hands on my back and ushers me back towards the stairwell. "Do you feel better now? It's not someone coming to kill us."

"No, it's just a bear who could rip our intestines out of our bodies with one swipe."

Dres doesn't respond and we trudge back upstairs and get back into bed quietly. Dres is radiating heat and I cling to it, curling up against his body. My feet are icicles so naturally I tuck them up into Dres's lap. He reaches down and rubs at my feet like he's using them to start a fire.

"So what's going on?" he asks. I can't really see him in the darkness of our room, which is nice because I know I'm making a face that just totally gives away how anxious I feel.

"Well you're rubbing my feet presently, which may be frost bitten."

"You can't be a doctor and be this wildly overdramatic."

"I'm a man of many talents."

He's staring at me hard. That I can tell even in the darkness. "You know what I meant."

I frown, taking my time to answer. "Okay, so I maybe worked myself up a bit."

"Yeah, a bit," he agrees. "But why?"

"I just got to thinking about your shoulder, which made me think about your arm. And, you know, up until you, I'd never met anybody who'd been shot before. And now you've been shot twice." I sigh loudly. "Look, I know we never really talked about this. But that night you came into my ER? That really fucked me up. And I felt like I couldn't even really express how hard it was to see you like that."

"I'm sorry," Dres says.

I pull my feet away so I can shift closer to him. There's just enough light that I can see his eyes, the shadow of his nose and the ring in his nostril. I focus on the gentle curve of his lips. "You don't have to be sorry," I say quietly. "You just have to be more conscious of the fact if you die you're killing me, too, so. And that's not me being overdramatic. I'm serious. I can't handle you rolling into my ER again."

"Alright, I'll let the EMTs know from now on I exclusively go to University only."

"Dres, I'm serious."

"I know." He touches my face, thumb brushing along my jaw. "I'll be more careful."

"Thank you."

The day I decided to stop writing Dres, I was sitting in an advanced psychology class. It was the middle of the summer before my last year at school. I'd started taking classes during my breaks Sophomore year to finish as quickly and as early as possible. I hated college. I think I would've hated college even if all of the things that went down between Dres and I hadn't gone down.

My class had a tendency to veer off topic. I liked those kinds of classes best, felt like it suited my learning style more than being lectured at for an hour and a half. Professor Rosenthal, who preferred we call them Jamie, was telling us the story of how they'd come out to their family. Jamie had been raised in rural Arkansas. Their parents flat out refused to accept any of the changes Jamie was asking of them, and never used their preferred pronouns. Eventually, Jamie said they had to accept that things weren't going to change. Despite how much they loved their family, they couldn't hold out hope that they could be the people who deserved to be in their lif e.

It was a hot day in California and sweat was pooling everywhere it could on me — the back of my neck, my palms, the crooks of my elbows and backs of my knees. I was counting down the seconds class would be dismissed and I could take my board to the beach.

Then Jamie said, "There comes a time, maybe many times, where you're going to have to turn your back on someone you love. You're going to need give up the belief that things will change, particularly when they've given you no indication that it will. You have to make the choice to move on and keep making it everyday until eventually, you start making it without thinking. Until eventually it stops feeling like you're making a choice at all."

For obvious reasons, it resonated.

At that point, I'd written Dres more letters than I should ever really own up to — all of which had gone unanswered. I'd told Dres about my life here, keeping him up-to-date on college, swimming, my surfing progress, even a few dead-end dates. I'd sent those mostly to see if I could even get a jealous angry letter back but I got nothing.

And then Jamie quoted to us, "Letting go means coming to the realization that some people are a part of your history, but not a part of your destiny."

And maybe it was the heat or dehydration or the fact I would be graduating school next year and transitioning into the next phase of my life but I knew they were right. Or I wanted them to be right. I wanted it enough that I decided I wouldn't send any more letters. I would write Dres one last time just to say I was finally letting him go.

Staring at Dres in this moment, with the stitch between his eyebrows and his dark lashes fanned against the tops of his cheeks, it's crazy to think that there was a chance we'd never be together again.

Maybe letting go means realizing that if someone's your destiny, they'll find their way back to you.

CHAPTER FOUR; part one

- -

C alvin Sumner

I wake and I've forgotten where I am.

And I have no idea what woke me until I smell it. Something syrupy sweet, something fried and doughy. I could be waking in the middle of a state fair.

I'm not, though. I'm in our bed and Dres is not. I roll onto my side, spreading my arm across the space where he should be. I have no idea what time it is. It's definitely not early. I feel rested, really rested. Sated, too. Just on the right side of sore. My muscles are sinfully strained.

I think about last night, about coming home. The disorientation that accompanies reuniting with someone you've been missing so much.

I think about the heated quickness of fucking against the front door, offset by the slow and agonizing way Dres buried himself inside me after we had napped. A sort of sleepy sex, like we weren't quite awake and were finding our way to each other in our dreams. Dres had sprawled himself across me, lying so perfectly in line that every part of me was touching him, every part but his mouth that hovered over mine so I could swallow his quiet moans as he sank into me and stayed like that for too long. Long enough that I had to whine and nip at his mouth to get him to move. It was all the contempt I could manage, since he had my arms pinned above my head, his fingers laced through mine.

Dres always liked to slow things down, to make me feel it, ache with it, with him. Like I needed any sort of reminding the power he had over me. Slow asked for a certain amount of control I didn't have when I was around him. He watched me the whole time, his eyes wide, the blacks of his pupils nearly absorbing all of the light. I wanted to know what was going on in that head of his. I wanted to ask him if it was good. I just wanted to say something, anything, to break the spell, to pull us back a bit, because we weren't there anymore.

But I didn't say anything. I just took it, all of him, in the slowest and deepest way he could give it to me. We're tethered, destined to go on forever even after it was over.

Dres didn't move right away when he finished, when we both had. I had tremors in my legs so I was in no hurry, either, trying and failing to find air in the small space between us. The release had bought an onslaught of sleepiness and so I started to rest my eyes, just for a minute. He moved his head, pressing his cheek against mine so he could sing our song into my ear, the one I'd played for him outside his door during quarantine, so soft I could've missed it if we hadn't silenced the universe already.

Whenever you need me, I'll be there.

It was a sort of love making that doesn't end even when the sex does, an intimacy that sticks. A moment that would flash before my eyes as I died so I could take the feeling with me into my afterlife.

I'm still thinking about it, replaying the night like it's a fantasy I created and have lived in my dreams, when Dres comes up the stairs. My eyes are closed so I don't see him, but I can hear his steps, however soft they are. I keep my eyes shut and he pads over to the bed. His weight shifts the mattress. I feel his breath near the side of my neck, and then he says my name right into m y ear.

"Cas." He nudges at my jaw with his nose. It's more like a nuzzle, feels strangely primal, and wakes more than my conscious. And then, "Baby, wake up."

I was prepared to jump this man in that moment.

So I do, naturally, turning swiftly and pressing my lips to the first bit of skin I can reach. I land on Dres's chin, shifting upwards to kiss his mouth next. He pulls away saying, "How'd I know that'd wake you up?"

"Petitioning for that to be the only way you wake me up from here on out," I retort reaching out to caress his face. "Although, to be fair, I was already awake."

"Why didn't you come downstairs?"

"I just wanted to lay here and enjoy myself for a bit."

His eyes dart down my body suggestively. "Without me?"

"I would make some joke about how I'm thoroughly spent, but we know that's not true," I say and Dres laughs with a small nod. The sound vibrates against my hand and I move it, running my fingers through his hair. It's still damp from the shower he's clearly had. I wonder, again, how long he's be en up.

Instead of asking, I say, "I slept so good last night."

I bring my hand back down to trace the curve of his ear, resting against his cheek, and Dres turns, kissing into my palm. It's a small gesture but it's how I know he's pleased. Dres buys stock in the little things — me getting enough sleep, me eating properly, taking care of me.

"Come downstairs when you're ready," he says pushing away from the bed.

I stare at him suspiciously, sitting up as I say, "What did you do?"

He shrugs casually. Forced casually. The same casual shrug he always gives when he's done something. "You'll have to see for yourself."

His expression remains neutral, giving nothing away.

I jump out of bed, rushing towards the bathroom so I can get downstairs and find out what he's done, wondering how he's even managed to do anything in the middle of a quarantine. When I finish in the bathroom and return to the room, Dres has made the bed and is no longer upstairs.

"Don't look," Dres calls from downstairs. "Just come down."

More suspicious than ever, and thinking about how dry and cracked my cuticles have been with all the hand washing, I head downstairs only to find the living room blacked out. Dres has covered the windows with dark blankets. The only light in the room is coming from the TV.

It illuminates the coffee table where there's a breakfast sprawl of fresh fruit, French toast, eggs, and bacon. Dres is standing at the end of the couch with my xbox controllers in his hand.

"So I'm proposing," he says and I nearly fall over my feet at the bottom of the stairs. "That we have the laziest day imaginable," he finishes, holding out the controller to me.

So not proposing, I realize. Not really.

"I love everything about this," I respond, walking over to take the controller from him. He sits and I take the other side of the couch. I do love everything about it, especially knowing how hard it is for Dres to write off a day completely. Laziest day imaginable to him would still involve banging out a quarter of his to-do list.

"My favorite," I say reaching for a slice of French toast.

Some of the syrup drips down my chin and Dres leans over, licking the line of it back to my mouth. "My favorite," he says quietly, voice sounding more like a purr. He's giving me eyes that aren't suitable for the general public.

So maybe not the laziest day imaginable.

The next three weeks consist mainly of this — Dres and I on the couch, and the counter, and the coffee table at one point, too. We do take a break from breaking furniture to drive up to the lake house and start furnishing it. "I need new options," I had told Dres the night before we left. We were entangled in bed, legs lapped over each other, the sheets pushed down to our ankles. The thrum of the central air was our only background noise.

"New options?" Dres had repeated, voice drowsy. He was always sleepier after I fucked him, like the less work took more energy. Although, to be fair, it often felt like when I topped that Dres was still the one doing the fucking.

"Yeah, we've banged on every piece of furniture in this place. I need a change of scenery. We also didn't do it in the hot tub and I think that was a missed opportunity."

"I'm not getting in the hot tub in this heat. It's been over ninety for the past three days. I would rather die."

"I love this weather."

"You also take showers at a temperature that should come with a warning label."

"Oh hardy-har-har."

"Hardy-har-har?"

"That's my you're not funny laugh."

"It's not even a laugh. It's words."

"Exactly, because you're not funny."

"I think you secretly think I'm hysterical."

"I secretly think lots of things about you."

"It's no secret you imagine me naked, Cas."

That time, I had laughed.

Dres was falling asleep on my arm, his chin tucked near my chest. I looked down at him and said, "What if we make the lake house like super gay? Over the top, just like gaudy, you know? Think Jeffree Star's home." I liked it better, I thought, when I fell asleep first. I'd get distracted watching him sleep otherwise.

He grumbled, "I'll no sooner set the place on fire."

"Zebra print."

"Whatever you want," he said next.

"Okay, so the Jeffree Star style."

"Except that."

"An homage to Cher."

"Okay."

"Can I commission an artist to paint me nude and then hang the portrait in the living room?"

There was a pause and then, "No."

"So much for anything I want."

Dres opened his eyes then, tilting his head up to look at me. I was grinning. "No one gets to see you naked but me."

"Ah, there's the Fifty Shades I know and love."

CHAPTER FOUR; part two

D resden Gibson

Cas makes good of his word, though it's a year later and so much has happened that I've forgotten he made the declaration. A surprise attack back, a surprise so huge I don't see it coming. It isn't a holiday, or a birthday, or an anniversary. Just a random day in September. Things are not normal, but they're the closest they've been to normal since the start of COVID-19 and the ensuing quarantine.

I re-opened Weston's in July for takeout and mobile ordering, but it was a slow start. I started doing takeout for Weston's After Hours every Saturday to both give me something to do and increase the revenue. For the better part of July and August, I was barely making ends meet with the store.

Things got better towards the end of the summer, enough that I could resume normal hours and Rumi and Tasha could return. Rumi's a senior now, but her high school is fully remote, so she's been here a lot. I let her do her zoom classes in the break room. This last years been hard on her. She lost her mother, grandmother, and two aunts to coronavirus.

Tasha and I have tried our best to be there for her, but she's a grieving teenager. It seems like everything I say to her is wrong. She doesn't want sympathy, and she doesn't want to be coddled, but when I try to talk to her casually, I get choked up remembering that her mother isn't going to be there to see her graduate. That she lost several female figures in her life in one fell swoop.

I realize that I'm not going to be able to ease her pain. You can't make someone happy when they're grieving. All you can really do is be there, quietly, readily, for when they need you.

Not that it matters, because Cas shows up and he rains the sun down on her sadness. Rumi isn't Rumi unless Cas is in the room. He has a way with her that I just don't understand, but continue to be amazed by. He even manages to get a laugh out of her sometimes.

I love him for lots of reasons. This has become one of them.

It's Friday, so I'm out grocery shopping. Cas makes fun of my routine. He also makes fun of how often I go grocery shopping, which is sage coming from the guy eating me out of house and home.

When I get home, I cook dinner, a simple rosemary chicken with some roasted potatoes because I'm tired and want something that's quick and easy. It's plated and ready for when Cas gets home. I always wait to eat dinner with him.

I've just gotten out of the shower when I get a notification that the alarm at Weston's has been tripped. In all the years I've had Weston's, I've never had any problems with the alarm system.

The alarm company calls me next. They ask for the code and I give it but explain I'm not there and am not sure if it's a false alarm or not. They let me know they'll be dispatching police. I call Cas as I get into my car and start making my way to the store.

"Hey," he answers. "I'm on my way home. Whats up?"

"The alarm got tripped at Weston's. I'm headed there."

"Do you want me to meet you there?" he asks.

"No, I'm sure it's nothing. The alarm people dispatched police. I'll call you when I get there if anything's up. But head home. You had a long day."

He yawns as if to reaffirm it. "Alright, keep me updated, please."

I beat the police to Weston's. The alarm's off and there's no sign of forced entry. There's lights on, though, in the back of the building, which I can see from the front door. They're dim, so maybe the kitchen lights. I wouldn't be able to tell from here if someone broke into Dolores's office, which is where we keep the safe.

I try the front door, but it's definitely locked. I unlock it and step inside, cautious even though it doesn't feel like there's any threat. Unless someone broke in through the back door, which is more likely.

I hesitate for a moment before continuing on. In the back of my head, I know I should wait. Wait for police to show up and secure the building. Wait for any sign that this isn't a burglary or someone planning to shoot me again. Cas would want me to wait. He's going to wring my neck when he finds out I didn't.

I don't wait, though. Maybe because I'm stubborn or maybe because I don't feel threatened. I feel uneasy, like I'm itching at a memory. Had I left the lights on when I left? Had Dolores come back and forgot to turn them o ff?

I proceed quietly through the main room into the back. My heart thrums in my neck, quick and heavy, making my jaw ache. It isn't fear. It's antici-pation. The thing right before the fear hits. The unease of not knowing.

One glance down the hallway tells me no one's opened the back door. The locks are still turned. Unless they locked it after themselves. Dolores's office is closed and when I try the door, it's locked.

There's light coming from a doorway at the other end of the hall. The door's open, which is not typical since it leads to the second floor and only the landlord has the key to access it.

I thought about leasing the space once, when I was playing around with the idea of opening my own restaurant, playing around with the idea of a more permanent After Hours. That was before the pandemic. Before the state put restrictions on indoor dining. Now it feels like a far-away idea. One that exists in a world where there isn't a deadly virus running rampant and people aren't scared to sit in a crowded room without a mask on.

Maybe someone else is leasing the space. I would think the landlord would have let me know that information, given the access they'd have to my own place, or that they'd simply use the outside entrance.

"Hello?" I call up the stairs, waiting a moment for a response before I start up them. The stairs creak under my weight. It's a narrow stairwell and there aren't any lights in it. Looking up at the top, I don't think there are any lights on in the room either.

My palm presses against my pocket where my phone is sitting, just in case.

I get to the top and the space opens, large and finished, dimly lit by industrial-style light fixtures with vintage filament bulbs hanging from the high ceilings.

It's Weston's, but it's not.

It's been modeled after Weston's, with the same stained woods and black accents. There's a large kitchen in the back of the room, visible over a half-wall that separates it from the dining tables. The tables have been arranged around the room in a variety of sizes, seating four, seating six, even some long buffet-style tables that could hold large parties or a be communal style of dining. But only one table has been set, a table for two.

Which is where Cas is standing, grinning at me hesitantly.

He's not in his scrubs or the clothes he wore into work today. He's wearing a suit that's grey, almost blue. The windowpane design is very subtle on it. The shirt he's wearing underneath is definitely blue, but maybe closer to purple, and his tie, like his belt and loafers, are charcoal. These aren't pieces from his closet. They're new. I've never seen him dress quite like this before, so daring and stylish, like someone dressed him.

When I meet his gaze, he smiles and says, "Surprise."

He holds up his hand, pressing down on the button in it and the room is illuminated in a warm yellow light as the sign behind him, that hangs above the open kitchen, lights up.

Weston's After Hours, it says.

"What?" I start to say but it's more a jumbled sound than anything.

Cas is still grinning. It's big, taking up most of his face. He's certainly pleased with himself. "Told you I was gonna surprise attack you back."

It's a restaurant. My restaurant. Cas bought me my restaurant.

"I did surprise you, right? You're surprised? Because this was the hardest secret to keep. No one should have to keep a secret so huge for so many months. I think I gave myself an ulcer."

I gasp. "Months?"

Cas keeping a secret for minutes is a feat.

"Months," he repeats with emphasis. "I started construction at the end of May. God, and then you opened back up in July and that fucked me up. Do you know how hard it is to get people to do construction at night?"

"May?"

"It was pretty clever, right, with the alarm company calling you. That was actually Lucy. And I knew, I totally knew you'd check the place out before the police got here, which we're going to have a conversation about later, Dresden Gibson. Your self-preservation skills are sorely lacking. And—"

Cas stops because I've crossed the room and pulled him to me, kissing him as hard as I can, a thank you and I love you wrapped in one breath.

"Hi," he says sort of breathless as he looks up at me. "Surprise."

I rest my forehead against his. "Huge surprise."

He's grinning again. "One could even say monumental."

"One would be right." I kiss him again, my brain and body trying to catch up with this moment. That I'm standing here with him in my restaurant. That Weston's After Hours is a real restaurant now. "I can't believe you did all this."

"I also made us dinner," he says, gesturing with a nod towards the table. "Broke in your kitchen for you. Emphasis on the broke. Not sure the oven survived."

My eyes dart to the table where the meals are covered with metal lids. "Is it edible?"

"Oh hardy-har-har." He gives me a shove, stepping back. I reach out for him, wanting to pull him back in but he steps out of reach. I turn my head curiously. He says, "I want you to pursue your dreams."

"Okay," I respond quickly. If Cas wanted me to quit my dreams, I'd do it for him. Asking me to live them out is not an ask.

"I want you to pursue them with me." He presses his hands into his chest.

My stomach swirls. The good kind of swirl. The nervous kind of swirl. "I want that, too."

"Okay, good. Then we're on the same page."

"We are."

"Because a lot can change in a year," Cas says. "Nothing is guaranteed." He knows that better than anyone. He's seen it firsthand.

I look at him, trying to figure out what he isn't saying. Cas gives nothing away. His expression is cool, like we're talking about the last episode of The Boys we watched.

"But also," he says softly. "A lot can not change in a year, in five years. Like the way I feel about you. Actually, if my feelings are changing it's only because they're getting stronger. Which is crazy because if they get any stronger the force of it may start knocking planets out of orbit."

I laugh, but it's a low sound that doesn't detour Cas. He's lamenting, the way he has a tendency to do. It is one of the most endearing things about h im.

He's still an arms length away, keeping the distance between us that is not nearly a distance. But I want him close. I want to hold him. When he starts saying things like this, I go mad with wanting him.

He says, "The entirety of me loves the entirety of you. All of you. Even the things that drive me nuts. Especially the things that drive me nuts. Like that you waltzed into a building that might have been broken into without waiting for police."

"It seemed safe," I say, trying to defend myself. He ignores me, trucking on.

"I love how hard you worked on Weston's. I love how hard you worked on yourself. Which I didn't miss, okay? I see you. And I see the way you take care of others. I love that about you, too. I love the way you take care of me. I can't say that loud enough. Can't express just how much it means to me, because you do, you're constantly taking care of me and I am—I am so grateful, Dres, to be on this journey with you. I'll never not be grateful and I'll never want to not be apart of it."

"I have no intentions of living this life without you again," I tell him honestly.

Cas smiles, and it's a smile that tells me he knows that, that he's not worried. Which is good because if there was anything I feared most about our past, it was not so much that Cas couldn't forgive me, but that he'd never be able to trust me again. To have someone's trust again after breaking it — it's not something you ever stop thinking about, it's not something you ever stop being thankful for or that you'll ever take for granted. It's no small thing.

"Well you don't have to," Cas says quietly that I almost don't even hear it.

I think he's trying to say something important. I'm suddenly very aware of everything — the candles, fancy table setting, that Cas is wearing a suit, that I'm not. I'm wearing his sweatpants, so they're ill-fitting and a tee shirt I'd just grabbed as I was running out of the house. Also his, I realize as I glance down. There's a pickle Rick on my chest and Cas is saying too much that I want to get on my knees for him, prayer to this feeling, sanctify this mo ment.

Cas takes a breath and then he says, softer than before, "Tonight's not just about the future of Weston's. It's about the future of us, too. Because when I think about what my life will look like five years from now — I don't see it ."

He pauses there like this needs to sink in. It doesn't. I've heard him loud and clear and I'm confused as ever.

"When I think about our life, though, five years from now...we're happy and maybe we have kids and a new house and—."

I cut him off.

I say, "So then marry me."

Cas goes still, goes quiet, mouth falling open into a delicate oh. It lasts all of one second before he shrieks, "Are you kidding me?"

I stare, surprised.

He shoots forward, slugging me in the arm. It's like a love tap, if anything. "You did not just hijack my proposal. You stole my freaking line!"

So that's what this is. I fight back a grin as I say, "I mean, to be fair, you weren't really getting to the point."

"Getting to the point?" he repeats. "I was trying to give a huge romantic speech to segue into my proposal. One you could tell our kids about and be like yeah, your dad is so poetic."

"More like long-winded."

"I'm going to revoke my proposal in five seconds."

"I mean technically you didn't propose, I did."

"Well take back your proposal because this is my proposal and it's going down in history as me proposing to you, not the other way around." Before I can even respond, Cas moves, getting down on one knee.

"You don't have to," I start to say because him on one knee makes me shaky, destroys me, even though it doesn't change not a thing.

He reaches for my hand, saying, "Dresden Gibson, chronic pain in my ass and best thing to ever happen to me and incidentally my dick as well, I fully intend to spend the rest of my life with you. Whether you like it or not, you're now saddled with me. But honestly, lucky for you because I'm aging like fine wine."

I don't say anything, staring at him, aware of every feeling rushing through me. Aware of the overpowering need to take him right here. To forego the engagement altogether and consummate the marriage right now.

"This is the part where you say aging more like a cheese, or something," Cas says clumsily.

"I love you," I say instead.

"Okay or you can say that," he mutters. "You're making me nervous looking at me like that. It's throwing me off."

"You have five seconds to finish and then I'm taking you on the floor right there."

Cas's eyes get wide and he mumbles the quietest "well fuck me" shaking his head as he reaches into the pocket of his jacket with the hand that's not holding mine. He has a ring box, that he opens against his thigh and then holds up to me. Inside is a thick ring, with three rows of little diamonds that are bright against the white gold band.

"Marry me," he says.

I drop suddenly to my knees in front of him, nodding my head. "Yes," I say. "Yes, Cas, I will marry you." Cas is pushing the ring down my finger but the five seconds are fully up so I'm pushing him back towards the ground.

"But the food," he says as I crawl over him. He tilts his chin, looking up at me. I've got his legs pinned with mine. "It'll get cold."

"We can reheat it," I say undoing the buttons on his jacket.

"I made chicken parm," he says and I pause.

"Like..." I trail.

"The first time we cooked together," he finishes.

It guts me. I can't hold myself up anymore, dropping so my head is in Cas's shoulder. There is nothing more we need — not rings, not a ceremony, not paperwork. I could not be any more married to this man than if God tethered our souls together.

"Are you okay?" Cas asks quietly. I nod as he strokes the back of my head soothingly. "Because you're crying."

"I'm just a little overwhelmed, " I say once I've caught my breath, turning my face so I'm pressed against his cheek. I breathe in, deep. He smells like rain, like a soft citrus with something dark and earthy under it.

"What parts overwhelming?" he asks.

"All of it."

He takes a breath and then goes, "Like in a too much, too fast, too soon kinda way?"

"Not too fast, not soon enough kinda way."

"But it is too much?"

I go quiet because it is too much but I wouldn't want it any other way. "When you walked in Westons, that first time, when Dolores hired you. You were so — you. It was like you filled the room with you. I couldn't take a breath without sucking you in, too. It scared the shit out of me. And it still scares the shit out of me. I think it's always going to."

"Well, I know that must be true because you're cursing," Cas says and we laugh.

"I've run from my fears before, but I don't plan to ever again," I say finally and Cas goes silent, turning to find my gaze. I've said it in the most solemn way I know how.

"I like to think that the universe conspired to bring us together."

"I'd like to agree," I say feeling my heart rate return to something close to normal. Cas is right. I was crying and my cheeks have that tight feeling where the salt has dried. "So what are we doing? Fucking or eating?" I ask after another moment.

"How are you going to ask me to choose between my two favorite things. That's like Sophie's choice. I mean obviously we're fucking but how dare you put me in this position where I actively have to—"

I kiss him to silence him thinking I've got a lifetime ahead of me with this long-winded man.

CHAPTER FIVE; part one

C alvin Sumner

It hasn't been like this in almost a year now.

And even when it was like this, it wasn't completely like this because Dres and I weren't together. We were something, but it wasn't concrete. Not like it is now. No, it was more like we were orbiting each other and playing Tetris with our moons, unsure we'd ever shift back into each other's atmospheres again.

The last time we had everyone, my whole family, and Dres's, and Jacks's, all together was the Thanksgiving before the pandemic. The night that took a significant turn for the worst but was also pretty pivotal in getting Dres and I to this point.

There was a moment where I thought — where I was really convinced that I would never be with Dres again. Not in the way that I wanted, anyway. It almost feels like a magic trick that that time of my life exists in the same universe as this time of my life. A life where I'm living with Dres and we're engaged.

I just — I think I'll always be amazed that we made it here. That everything that happened between us worked in tandem to bring us together.

Tonight we're celebrating, but our family doesn't know it. They think this is just a barbecue, one where we can catch up in the ways zoom calls failed to allow in the last six months.

It's so nice having everyone together again that it actually slips my mind there's a reason they're here. The conversation is steady, bouncing from light topics like the Toilet Paper Crisis of March to heavier ones, like the social injustices surrounding the murders of George Floyd and Breonna Taylor and then the looming anticipation of the coming election and the constant unrest that is our country.

But then we swing back to lighter topics because it's been a year of heaviness and we just need to have a laugh. Despite what Dres says, I provide the much needed comedic relief.

I'm so distracted in my story telling that I don't notice how late it's gotten until Dres stands and goes, "Is everyone ready for dessert?"

The question halts me and my body hums with anticipation.

"That's a trick question," I say to the table. "Because if you guys don't eat whatever he's baked, I will. And quarantine twenty is cute thick, but anything more and I'm gonna' need new scrubs."

Dres frowns. "You didn't even gain twenty pounds."

"This dump truck I'm carrying around would beg to differ."

Beside me, Amelia cackles. Jack grimaces and goes, "Everything about that sentence is wrong."

Across the table my mom makes this face that asks me why are you like this?

The simple answer is Tiktok. I'm currently in the process of making my super hot fiancé famous. I even coined the best freaking username: dessertswithd. I lied and told Dres the 'd' stands for his name but come on. I am nothing if not consistent and it's a well known fact how I feel about certain Dresden appendages.

"I'd actually like you all to be my cake testers for the evening. I'm doing something different. I have some time, though, so no decisions need to be made on the flavor tonight."

I say, "Normally this is a position only I hold, but I'm willing to share it just this once."

Dres winks at me.

Down the table Dolores is dubious. "Since when do you care about any-one's opinion of your cakes other than Cas's?"

I can't help but grin. Six years and some things do, in fact, stay exactly the same. It's good to know we're all on the same page in that I am the mastermind behind the cupcake flavors.

"You're right," I say. "He's only offering this as a courtesy. I'm ultimately going to be the deciding voice."

"Well I'm dumb full," Amelia says flinging herself backwards in her chair so she can put her belly on display for the table, exposed in a tiny crop top and loose chiffon pants. "But I'm not going to turn down dessert."

"What's this new flavor?" my mom asks glancing over at Dres.

"Let me go get it," Dres says instead of answering, turning on his heel and walking back inside. Charlie waits point five seconds before getting up from his spot in the shade and following Dres into the house. Delta's at my feet, and while she lifts her head curiously for a second, she drops it down on my feet again, unmoving.

"So Cas," my grandmother says. "How is homemaker life going?"

"I'm sorry homemaker? I think the more accurate term is home wrecker. I broke the washer machine last week and flooded the hallway." A true and sad fact, especially when I was expressly forbidden from doing the laundry.

Maddox manages to lift his head from his Nintendo switch long enough to laugh at me. Of course he finds that funny.

"Oh no," Aunt Suki says. "How did that happen?"

"Well," I respond with a flourish of my hands. "Washing machines capacity should be directly in line with how much it can physically fit. This isn't a Starbucks. Why am I leaving room at the top?"

"Cas," my mom says, aghast. To be fair, she did the laundry the whole time we lived together so if anyone's to blame for my ineptitude. I'm not pointing fingers but if I were....

"On the bright side," I say. "The lake house is fully furnished finally. Took all summer but I nailed it. So maybe we'll do Thanksgiving there this year."

Grandma regards me fondly, her eyes getting a little watery. "It feels like just yesterday you were this little thing throwing temper tantrums every time anyone put you in floaties at the pool and now you're this doctor with a whole life and home and." She stops, getting choked up.

"See now this is the reaction I expected from you when I moved out, mom."

"I'm feeling grateful you moved out before you got your hands on my washer machine."

"I told you guys this in confidence," I say but we're all laughing. See Dres, I think pointedly. Comedic relief.

"Don't you know nothing is sacred in family," Amelia jeers. She says it like we're family, her and I. And I know we are, and will be on paper soon enough, too. But for her to say that without knowing means more. I always felt it was important to get along with Dres's family, but I never had to actually work to do that with Amelia. Dolores, either, but Amelia and I get along like we would've been friends even if she wasn't Dres's sister.

"Dres, what's the hold up?" she calls out. "My food baby needs replenishing and it's getting cold out here."

I glance over at the back door and can see Dres through the screen. He has a cake platter in one hand and uses the other to get the door. I shift my hands to my lap, slipping one into my front pocket to remove my ring and slide it down my pointer finger. It's discreet enough that Amelia doesn't notice, but then she's too busy blowing into her hands.

Once the sun set, the temperature dropped the way it does in the fall and Amelia can't be getting any warmth from the thin shirt she's wearing. I want to grab her a jacket but I have to wait for Dres. He has a whole thing planned.

Everyone's distracted at the table so they don't notice him at first when he walks up, the cake balanced on his hand. It's white and two-tiers, with clusters of flowers and ribbon designs and there's a cake topper of two men in black and white tuxes. There's no mistaking this for anything but a wedding cake.

Amelia's the first to notice Dres. "Wait—what?" she says, her expression confused.

The table goes silent as everyone turns to stare at Dres. I refrain from laughing, knowing how much he just loves the spotlight on him.

Dres keeps a neutral expression as he returns to his seat across from me at the center of the table and places the cake in the middle.

"Is that a wedding cake?" Jack asks, breaking the silence.

"Obviously that's a wedding cake," Jasmine mutters.

"Why are you baking a wedding cake?" Dolores goes.

I meet my mom's gaze. She's right next to Dres, but she's not looking up at him like everyone else. She's staring at me. Her expression is a mix of confusion and shock. She says slowly, "Calvin, are you..."

But Amelia goes loudly, "Okay, but why are we taste-testing a wedding ca—ah, oh my god! Is this your wedding cake?"

She reaches for my hand, the way I suspected she would, pulling my arm above the table. "You're engaged?" she screams. She turns to Dres. "You're getting married?"

Dres's eyes are on me as he nods. "We're getting married."

I'm startled by Amelia who throws her arms around my shoulders, squeezing me into her chest. "Oh my god, oh my god," she says but her voice is drowned out by the rest of the table turning into a frenzy. Congratulations come from both ends, from everybody. In the corner of my eye I see my mom get up and hug Dres tightly. She says something over his shoulder but I don't hear her.

I pat Amelia's back, trying to pull away. "We're going to be siblings," she says.

"In-laws," Dres corrects. How he even heard her, I don't know.

"Semantics," she responds.

I manage to untangle myself from her embrace, getting up so I can make my way over to my mom. Suki and Dan intercept me before I can get to her. Suki pulls me into a hug as she plants a kiss on my cheek.

"Does this mean Dres is my cousin, now too?" Maddox asks not glancing up from his game.

"It does," Suki says pulling away. "We're all family now."

"Nice," Maddox says. "Now I have a cool cousin."

"Wow, shots fired. I'm going to remember that," I say as I pass Suki to get to my mom who's waiting.

She opens her arms to me and I sink into her, breathing in the person I spent the first part of my life with. "I've been dying to tell you," I say my voice muffled in her shoulder.

She laughs. "I'm amazed you managed not to," she says. "Congratulations."

"Thank you."

She squeezes my shoulders and then pushes me back so she can look up at me. "I am so proud of you." Her words come slowly as she fights back tears. If she cries, I'm going to cry and that's not going to be cute.

I laugh, uneasily and ask, "Because I'm getting married?" She shakes her head, letting me go to brush away a stray tear.

"Because you're fearless."

The last thing I want to do is start crying but I say anyway, "If I'm fearless it's because I learned it from you."

That about does it and a few more tears escape that she lets fall. I hug her again, tightly. "This next part of your life, Cas," she says quietly into my ear. "Is going to be the best years of your life. But they go so fast. So enjoy every second of it. You deserve it."

Over her shoulder, I see Dolores with Dres. They aren't hugging, but I didn't expect them to. They've always had a strained relationship, better now than it's ever been according to Dres but still strained, nonetheless. Sometimes I wish Dres had what I have with my mom. Because what I have with my mom is special, is one of the best things about my life. I love her t o death.

But that's not Dres and Dolores. For their own reasons, their own faults, they can't get close like that. I don't discredit the ways in which they have tried, the strides they've made to meet each other.

Dolores holds Dres's face now and looks at him with nothing but warmth in her expression. She whispers something before she walks away and he's left there, smiling.

"Excuse me," I say pulling away so I can walk past her to get to him. I come up behind him, getting on the tips of my toes to lean over his shoulder.

"What'd she say?" I whisper and he noticeably jumps, turning around to me.

"That's personal," he says.

I grin. "Nothing's personal when you're married."

"Well we're not married yet."

"Semantics."

Dres steps closer, reaching up to tug on the collar of my shirt. "What'd your mom say?"

"She said she's proud of me," I tell him. "Because I'm fearless."

He purses his lips thoughtfully. "She's right."

"Uh, yeah, you know I didn't really feel all that fearless when I woke you up to kill a spider in the bathroom the other night."

"I actually have a confession," Dres says. "I never killed that spider."

I whack him in the arm. "Are you kidding me?" I scream. "I've been showering with a spider the last few days? Divorce. This is grounds for divorce."

Dres groans. "Oh god, is this what the next years going to be like? Are you going to divorce me when I tell you we're no longer getting oat milk, too?"

I stare, shocked. "Uhm, yes? Because why would we not get oat milk, anymore? Is this your ploy? Get me engaged and then pull the rug out from under me. Not killing spiders, no longer buying oat milk. This is a conspiracy."

"You literally never drink the oat milk."

I sputter. "I — what, that's simply just untrue."

Dres gives me a look. "I throw out the cartoon every other week. It's full. You have maybe a cup of it. And even that's generous."

"Well maybe I'm just leaving some for you. Because I'm a thoughtful husband. A caring husband. A husband who would not lie about killing a spider."

"But I drink almond milk."

"As nice as it is to listen to you two argue," Jasmine says interrupting us. "I think what we all really want to hear is the proposal story."

"Yes," Amelia exclaims. "We have to hear this story. Who proposed?"

Dres and I say at nearly the same time, "I did."

My grandfather looks over at us, confused. He's already helped himself to some cake and the spoon hovers near his mouth. "You both did?"

"Technically, it was Cas's proposal," Dres says.

"Yeah, that Dres hijacked." I give him a rather pointed look.

"Maybe if you didn't take your time getting to the point," he mutters and my mother, betrayer that she is, laughs.

I go, "I was trying to be romantic!"

"Admittedly, it was very romantic," Dres says.

"I'd probably agree," Amelia says. "If you'd tell us the dang story."

Uncle Dan grimaces but nods. "It would help to have some context."

Dres looks at me questioningly and I go, "You tell it," as I make my way back around the table to my seat.

I don't have to look to know he's uncomfortable with everyone's attention on him again. But his voice doesn't portray it as he starts. "So about three weeks ago—"

"You got engaged three weeks ago?" Dolores interrupts. Safe to say I know where Amelia gets it now.

I say, "We wanted to tell everyone together and, no offense, but none of you are easy when it comes to scheduling."

Dres trucks on. "It's a Friday night so Weston's closed early. I was at home when I got a call from the alarm company that the alarm had been triggered. They said they dispatched police but I started making my way over to check things out, anyway."

"And so he calls me," I say.

"Are you going to let me tell the story?" he questions.

Grinning, I say, "I'm helping provide context. Your phone call let me know things were in motion."

"Well, provide more context because I'm confused," Suki says.

"So I called Cas," Dres explains. "To let him know I was heading to Weston's to check out the alarm. When I get there, though, everything seems fine. Except there's lights on that I didn't leave on when I left. And police aren't in sight."

"Which," Dres adds quickly. "I know I should've waited for them but I didn't so please don't berate me."

Both Dolores and my mom have disapproving mom faces on but they do refrain from berating Dres.

"I go inside, into the back, and the light is coming from a stairwell that goes up to the second floor. That areas's not apart of my lease and as far as I knew no one had rented it out."

Dres pauses and meets my gaze over the table. His silence etches on and everyone at the table turns to look at him, waiting. His stare is all smoke, a stoked fire between us. I clear my throat and go, "So naturally, even though all signs point to an intruder being in Westons, Dres goes upstairs anyway."

"Which you banked on," he interrupts.

"You are predictably reckless with your life."

Amelia goes, "Which is a problem, might I add."

"This is the most convoluted story telling I've heard and I have toddlers," Jack remarks making the whole table laugh.

"So I go upstairs," Dres says with more conviction. "And the space is — it's like Weston's. It is Weston's, I realize. An extension of it, anyway. And Cas is standing under a sign that says 'Weston's After Hours' and he's got this huge, idiotic grin on his face."

"Excuse me, my grin is not idiotic!"

Dres clamps down on a laugh as he says, "The smug one you do is."

"Smug for good reason," I exclaim. "I've pulled off the surprise of the century. I'll have you know trying to pull one over on Dres is a near impossible feat. And I kept this secret for months. Months."

"Months?" my mom repeats. "That actually is a feat."

Amelia turns in her seat to look at me. "So wait, let me get this straight. Cas. You bought Dres a restaurant?"

"Well, I bought him the space for his restaurant."

"Semantics," Amelia says. "Absolute semantics."

Everyone is looking at me with weirdly soft expressions. I'm not one to really shy under the spotlight but this is a lot. I'm uncomfortable.

"Go big or go home," I say trying to make light of the situation. "Which is exactly what I was trying to do when I began my three part proposal speech."

"More like twelve page proposal dissertation."

I glare at Dres. "More like wildly romantic, insanely poetic—"

"Long-winded," he interrupts.

"It only feels long winded because you restrict yourself to six-word sentences."

"'So then marry me' is only four words."

I look back at the table and make a sweeping gesture towards Dres. "Evidently I was saying all the right things because right in the middle of this grand speech Dres says so then marry me. Like talk about beating a guy to the punchline."

"And so naturally Cas flips out on me."

I make a sound of dismay. "You usurped my proposal. Why wouldn't I flip out?"

"I like to think I expedited it," he says winking at me. "And anyway," he says to the table. "Once he was done yelling at me for stealing his moment he got down on his knee and said—"

"I don't think you should repeat everything I said."

"Knowing the things I know, I would have to agree," Jack says.

Amelia wrinkles her nose. "Ew."

Dres goes on anyway. "He says, Dresden Gibson, I am an exceptional specimen of man meat, you'd be insane not to lock this down."

I very nearly fall out of my seat. And so does my mom. She gasps and goes, "Cas, what in the world."

"That's not what I said," I practically scream, flushing. Except it sounds exactly like something I would say. Exceptional specimen of man meat? The line itches at my memory. How does Dres even remember that?

Dres grins. "No, what he really said was—"

I cut him off quickly, fearful of where he'll go this time. "What I really said was: Dresden Gibson," I look over at him, locking eyes with his in a stare that makes everything else around us disappear, "seeing as you got me pregnant—."

"Cas!" I can't even distinguish who at the table yells my name because I'm pretty certain everyone at the table is yelling my name. Jack and Amelia are laughing and even Jasmine, though she's pretending not to, hiding her mouth with her hand.

"Sorry guys," I say once everyone's calmed down. "But I think what I really said will stay between me and Dres. Just know that it was romantic enough to give Pablo Neruda a run for his money."

"I wouldn't say that," Dres says.

"Do you want me to tell them what happened after I proposed?" I retort and Dres flushes "Yeah, that's what I thought."

"You two are something else," Dolores says rubbing at her head.

"Something like a headache," my mom finishes.

Dres picks up a serving knife. "Alright, well I really would like your opinions on the cake. Its double chocolate with a cherry cream cheese filling."

And because we're siblings now, or nearly almost, I lean over and whisper to Amelia, "Dres is all about the cream filling."

Amelia squeals, shoving me. "Ugh, Cas, TMI!"

Dres shoots me a look. I raise my hands into the air. "I didn't say anything."

"That's disgusting. But also not surprising," Amelia mutters shaking her head like she can wipe the comment from her brain like an etch-a-sketch. "I now need enough alcohol to choke a horse." She reaches for the pitcher of sangria on the table.

Once she's filled her glass, she raises it and goes, "Alright, but in all seriousness. A toast to Cas and Dres. I'm so glad you both decided to stop being stubborn mules." It takes a moment for everyone to remove themselves from the slices of cake Dres has started doling out and raise their glasses. Amelia looks at me, her expression radiating warmth. "And I'll be honored to call you brother soon."

"What is soon, exactly?" my grandmother interrupts. "Have you picked a date?"

"Next year," I say and Dres nods. "Either end of May or beginning of June depending on the venue."

"That isn't as far away as you may think," my mom remarks. "You've got your work cut out for you. Especially finding time around your actual work."

"But that's why I have you," I jeer.

Our arms are still in the air. Uncle Dan goes, "All the details can be hashed out another time. To Cas and Dres."

We clink glasses before taking respective sips from them.

After cake, the oldest of us tap out. Goodbyes and more congratulations go around and then it's just us, Jack, and Amelia. Jasmine's left to relieve the sitter. Her and Jack argued over him staying. He insisted on going home with her but she was all that's your best friend, stay and celebrate. It was c ute.

But then I think that Jasmine's our friend, too. Cause that's what it means, right, when you're a couple. Your partners friends are your friends. I consider Jack a friend. But maybe I should make actual friends myself. I'm not even sure who I'll have in my wedding party. Lucy and I are friendly, but not friends, I would say. Like close coworkers. And I haven't spoken to Halston or Grace since my graduation.

"I have no friends," I realize, aloud.

Dres and Amelia look over at me. "You have friends," Amelia says but Dres doesn't. His silence actually confirms it for me.

"You have me," he says after a moment.

Between sips from my glass I say, "Amelia, I'm officially requesting your friendship."

"No," Dres says quickly. "No, you can't make that request."

"Sure he can," she snaps and then says fondly to me, "I accept."

"Great, be my best woman, then?"

"What? You can't ask my sister to be your best woman."

"But I just freaking did."

Jack nudges Dres with his foot. "Hey, why haven't you asked me to be your best man, yet? I'm offended."

"Jack, you can totally share the position with Amelia. I'll have the best of both genders."

Dres goes, "How are you going to steal my sister and my best friend?"

"I think it's only fair since you stole my proposal."

"Will I ever live this down?"

Jack goes, "I actually can't imagine you two married because you already act like you're married. Like is it going to be ten times worse for all of us watching or are you guys going to finally cool things down? Like are saunas going to be safe when they open back up?"

"The sauna?" Amelia exclaims.

I'm grinning and Dres looks over at me, noticing it, knowing what it means. "Don't say it," he warns but it's too late. I've thought it so now I've got to say it.

"I mean probably give me like a year to get all the married sex out of my system and then I should mellow out."

Dres groans, throwing his head into his hands.

I grin. "I love that we're family now and I can just—"

Dres cuts me off. "You can't."

I hold up my hand. "Hey did you guys know Dres's dick sorta leans..."

CHAPTER FIVE; part two

D resden Gibson

The first time Cas says it, I think he's joking.

I'm on the phone with Linden, our wedding planner, and I've been on the phone with him for an hour, trying to come to an agreement on the time-frame for the day. Linden is insisting on a later ceremony.

"You'll be facing the sunset and you'll be bathed in this glow when you exchange your vows. I'm telling you — it'll be absolutely magical."

"It sounds absolutely magical," I snap. "But it's not what I want."

It also does not work with my plans, plans of which I've yet to tell Cas about. It's not something I can spring on him the day of the wedding, though, so I'm going to tell him. A surprise, but one I'm willing to let stand on its own, without the tease of dinner and subtle comments like your passport is up to date, right? (It is, I checked with Olivia.)

Cas is unsuspecting, has been unsuspecting for weeks. He's on the couch now, watching Home Alone for the umpteenth time, even though Christmas is two weeks behind us. He's also refused to take down our Christmas tree, who's spilling needles everywhere like a popped piñata. And I'm nearly certain his diet has consisted only of those sugar cookies with the pictures of reindeer and Christmas trees and gingerbread men in the center.

Cas turns his head so he can look at me over the back of the couch, smirking as he says, "Okay, bridezilla."

I gape at him, pointing to my chest. "Me? A bridezilla?" I mouth quietly as Linden goes on and on about sunlight and glares in photos and sweating and golden hours.

"Yes, you," he says with a laugh. "What's a few hours later in the day?"

I turn my back to Cas and say to Linden, "We're doing the earlier ceremony. And it's final because invitations are already being printed."

Linden huffs and then caves, which he was always going to do. While he makes some valid points, and I could see the appeal of an evening ceremony, it doesn't work for the timeline. I've left a few hours for error but I'm not trying to dance in that window. Literally. The reception has a strict cut-off of nine p.m.

I hang up with Linden and join Cas on the couch, crawling up between his legs so I'm lying on his chest. He looks down at me as he reaches up and pushes my hair back.

"I don't think you and Linden are both making it to June 5th. It feels like a fight to the death," he says with a laugh.

"Well hopefully his death, otherwise you'll be at the alter alone."

"Huh, I don't know. I may be forced to take Linden's hand."

"I'll fire him."

Cas's chest vibrates as he laughs softly. "Don't be jealous," he says and then his expression shifts in a way I'm all too familiar with. "Or actually, yes be jealous. It's doing things for me."

"Everything does things for you," I respond, my tone teasing. "I could breathe and that would do it for you."

"You know most people would count their blessings to have a partner as responsive as me," he responds in too thoughtful a tone, all things considered. Like he has genuinely contemplated this.

This line of conversation only leads to one place and I can't get distracted. Not yet. "Where's your phone?" I ask him, shifting onto my side a bit because Cas is hard and feeling it against my chest is doing little to help with the whole distraction thing.

"Why?" he asks and then he grins. "Are we going to film it?"

"Film what?"

"Uhm, are we not about to fuck? I thought that was what this was leading to."

I bite back a grin. I love him but he does have a one-track mind. "Can you focus for five seconds?"

"I don't know. It's kind of hard. And by that I do, in fact, mean my dick — hey! Don't look at me like that. You're the one who crawled between my legs. I was happily watching Home Alone here."

"Cas," I groan dropping my head against his inner thigh.

"Oh, come on. I can hear it in your voice."

"Hear what?"

"You know what." His voice is low and all suggestion.

I huff and sit up, pushing myself out of his lap because he's right. It is in my voice but I need to tell him this one thing first and then. And then. Hm. "What do you want?" I ask him, moving to my knees so he has to look up at me from his reclined position. His leg are up and bracketing my hips. I rest my hands on his shins.

He smirks. "Take off your shirt," he says. "Slowly."

The way Cas enjoys watching me undress is not a new thing. It's not a thing I'll tire of, either. He's got that smoke screen look on his face now. I do the thing he loves, reaching behind my head for a fistful of fabric. I pull it up and over at a snail's pace and when its completely off I drop it on Cas's che st.

He licks his lips and then says, "Can you do it again but even slower?"

I tilt my chin at him. "Phone first."

"I don't know where that thing is," he whines shifting so he can shove his hand between the back cushions of the couch. "What is with you and my phone tonight? Do you want me to record you? Is tonight our introduction into exhibitionism because I think I need to shave first."

"You don't need to shave," I say seriously.

Cas rubs at his chin with his free hand while the other continues its descent into the couch cushions. "I'm stubbly. The curtains should match the drapes, I think."

"I like it."

"What, the curtains or the drapes?" he asks cheekily.

"The curtains and the lack of drapes," I respond.

"Aw, I'll tell Bianca you appreciate her work," he says with a wink. Bianca's his waxer and he has the kind of relationship with her that most men build with their barber.

Cas stops his search and I raise an eyebrow questioningly. "Did you find it?" I ask.

He pulls his hand out and holds his phone up. "Seriously why are you having me look for my phone right now when..."

"When what?" I ask when he doesn't finish.

Cas rolls his eyes and says in his most belittling tone, "When I obviously want you to fuck me, Dres, what else?"

"You're going to want me to fuck you more after you look at your phone."

Cas's eyebrows go up and then he scowls, nudging me with his knee. "Oh, I freaking knew it. I knew this was a thing. What did you do now? Christmas was like yesterday. If you keep surprising me with things I'm going to expect surprises all the time and do you know how exhausting that's going to be for you in twenty years?"

My heart rate picks up at the promise of twenty years because I want it. I want it so much.

"I'm never going to tire of surprising you, Cas," I tell him.

He shifts, sitting up so I'm no longer between his legs. I sit back on the heels of my feet, watching him. His phone's unlocked and I can see his mailbox with twelve notifications. "Maybe I'll fuck you," Cas says after a moment. "As a thank you. Would you like that?"

I'm hot. I'm hot all the time. I just run that way, but this is a different hot. Fire in my veins sort of hot, with desire as the kindling. My voice has dropped when I answer, "I'd like that."

"You're so pretty when you're all flushed," he says next, pressing his palm against the side of my face.

He's killing me and I'm too turned on to focus. Forget for a moment what we're supposed to be doing as I reach out and grab the waistband of his sweat pants, tugging them out of the way so I can slip my hand inside. I wrap my fingers around him but then I stop, holding him right where I want him.

"Check your email," I say remembering, somehow. Cas is biting his bottom lip, unfocused and trying not to be. I add, "I'm not moving my hand until you do."

"Okay, okay, I'm checking," he says in a rush. I watch him open his email. The one I forwarded to him is the second from the top. He taps it and his eyebrows scrunch together as he scans the contents. It's a ticket confirmation from EWR TO LHR departing at 11:10pm on June 5th.

"Dresden Gibson," he says finally and then he meets my gaze. He reaches out, clasping his hand around my forearm. He pulls my hand away so it's no longer in his pants and he's staring so wide-eyed at me I can't tell if it's good or bad.

I wait for his reaction. For any reaction.

There's no reaction, though, just Cas placing his hands on my shoulders. Cas, pushing me back till I'm lying with most of my body over the armrest. Cas, still not saying anything, staring at me with an expression that's unreadable. Cas, stretching my legs out for me like I'm a marionette doll.

"I can't tell if this is a good reaction or a bad one," I say when I've caught my breath.

"It's both," Cas responds as he fists the waistband of my pants and starts tugging them off.

"I love you so much," he says next and he could be talking about pizza, it comes out so easily. Less like an admission and more like an acknowledgment of facts.

"You are my favorite person," he says as he draws my briefs down. I lift my hips for him, hearing him but having a hard time registering his words.

"And you spoil me so much I wonder what sacrifices I made in another life to deserve this one with you." He looks up at me now and I can't not hear him, not when he's saying something so deeply honest, something he truly believes.

"You were always deserving of this life, Cas. Deserving of even so much more."

"You can't do anything more for me because I have no idea what I'll do back."

"You don't have to do anything back."

"Well, I'm still going to fuck you like your life depends on it."

"Please do," I say and it hits a whining note as Cas leans down and licks away the precum dripping down the length of me.

Cas draws back, looking up at me as he goes, "Can you reach the lube behind you?"

I shift onto my side, twisting so I can open the drawer on the side table and grab the lube's that's inside it. I don't even have to dig. It's the first thing on top.

It is both the most and least practical place to keep lube. We've had sex in this living room almost as much as we have in our bed so it makes sense. But Jack and Amelia have both stumbled across it, and while I was able to put Jack back in his place by recalling the recent can you look at my balls

I think I have testicular torsion event, Amelia had full grounds to Venmo request me $50 for emotional trauma.

Cas holds his hand out to me as he takes my length deep into his throat. I barely manage to slip the tube into his palm before I'm forced to clench the couch cushions. All the talking has teased me to the edge already. It's so good I don't want to stop, but it's so good I need to stop.

I don't have to say it, though. Cas can tell, knows my body as well as I know his, and pulls back, sitting up as he uncaps the bottle and pours some on his fingers. His mouth is cherried and wet, matching the blush on his cheeks.

He leans down, hovering over me as he slides his hand between my legs, working a finger in easy. I gasp from the sensation, so ready that my nerves are heightened. Cas catches the sound with his mouth, slipping his tongue inside letting me know what I taste like as he gets a second finger inside me

I lift my chin so I can get enough space between our mouths to say, "Cas." It's a plea, a request, and Cas meets my gaze, knowing it.

And yet he still goes, "Yes Dresden?"

I give him a look. He gives me a look back. All the while his fingers are curling upwards with so much good friction, I can barely see straight.

"Cas, please," I repeat because I can't take it and I'm using every last ounce of restraint not to finish.

Cas licks his way to the edge of my jaw, then dips his head to my ear, and goes, "Please what?"

My words leave me with my breath. "Fuck me."

Cas leans back, looking me in the eye as he squints and then says thoughtfully, "Mmm, I think you can ask nicer than that."

He's right, I can. And I know just what to say to get my way.

"Cas, baby, please fuck me."

He grins. Baby is the magic word, one I use sparingly. But if there's ever a situation that calls for it, it's this one.

He kisses the center of my neck as he removes his fingers, shifting so one of his feet is planted on the floor and his other knee is on the couch, pressed against my inner thigh. He's yanked his sweatpants down enough, but not completely off and he grabs my legs, opening them wider as he lines himself up.

"You're going to want to hold on," Cas says and he's right, I am.

He asked me to stop surprising him with gifts, but if he's going to fuck like this when I do, I'm just going to keep giving him everything I have and more.

We're lying in bed a few hours later and I'm falling asleep, perfectly wrecked, full on Cas and the grilled cheeses I made afterwards. Cas is on top of me, leg hooked over my hip and arm around my waist so that his body heat is my blanket. I thought after a month or two of living together it'd stop, this way of sleeping like we're trying to preserve the oxygen between us, but it hasn't after a year and I'm starting to think it never will. Which is fine so long as the thermostat is set low. But Cas prefers to swelter and likes to crank it up when he thinks I'm not looking.

He's doing this humming thing now, almost like a cat's purr. I can't tell if it's a post-sex thing or post-grilled cheese (I make a mean grilled cheese.) It's probably both.

He say suddenly, "Are you real?"

I smile up into the darkness and say, "I'm actually from the future. I was supposed to deliver a really important message but I got side-tracked."

Cas laughs but it's distant. He's in his head. "I can't believe you booked our trip. I thought we were kidding when we talked about it. You know, like a whimsical, pie in the sky kind of thing."

"If you want it, I'm going to do everything in my power to get you it, Cas."

He quiets for a moment. His breath is even against my chest and I half-think he's fallen asleep until he goes, "Okay, change of plans. Let's elope."

His comment forces a surprised laugh out of me. "You can't hold out for five more months?"

"I don't want to hold out for five months," he whines.

"If you still want to in the morning, we can," I tell him, very much dishonest.

"I know that's your lying voice."

"It's not," I say quickly and he sinks his teeth into my nipple, doesn't bite, just presses down like a threat. "Okay, look it's just — a lot goes into a wedding. A lot. And I'm..."

"Keep going." I can hear the grin in his voice.

"I'm excited for it."

"Aw."

"Stop it."

"Thats so cute."

"I mean it."

"So you're obviously going to walk down the aisle towards me," he says.

"You're so funny."

"I knew one day I'd get you to admit it."

"I was being sarcastic."

"Let the record show Dresden Gibson thinks I'm funny."

"Go to bed. You're intolerable."

As it turns out, Cas is right. I'm something of a bridezilla. It's as unprecedented for me as it is for Cas, who finds the whole situation hysterical. I'm on the phone constantly, hashing out details about flowers and color schemes, seating charts and music choices.

And as the wedding gets closer, my stress levels skyrocket. I'm developing a worsening need to micromanage everything. It doesn't help that I'm running both Private Weston's and Weston's After Hours mostly on my own. It's my intention to hire another chef and at least two sous chefs, but given the fact I'm going to be away all summer, it feels pointless to bring in staff just to have to let them go. It's not like I don't know it isn't sustainable, me running two businesses on my own, no matter how badly I may want to

.

While Cas and I are away all summer, After Hours will be closed and Private Weston's will be held down by Dolores, Charles, and Amelia. I'm actually not sure how much Amelia will be contributing since she offers very little skill in both baking and customer service. But she'll be house sitting and taking care of Delta and Charlie, which is way more important to me than having her help out at Weston's.

Cas was convinced we could somehow bring them abroad with us, and neither of us wanted to board them for the summer. It wouldn't have come down to that. Dolores and Charles would've taken them, but I much preferred Amelia staying at my place, instead. They've never been away from me for any period of time, really, so if I could maintain some routine for them I would try.

Cas, unsurprisingly, is zero help in the wedding planning process but he also notes that "if I did help you then you couldn't micromanage everything and what fun would that be for a bridezilla?"

He's never been good at planning things. It took him a whole week to plan a date with me just for us to spend the evening at his house (that evening I learned Cas had braces, emulated Justin Bieber, and hated losing in video games.) So it's not a shock that Cas can't and doesn't want to help with the wedding planning.

It does surprise me when one night he says, "I know you're not doing a bachelor night with Jack. Which I think is stupid."

It's Sunday night, we're in bed early, and it's less than one week to the wedding.

"As you've told me many times," I say, turning on my side to look at him.

He turns too, giving me a look that's like the precursor to an eye roll. He thinks I'm not doing a bachelor night because he doesn't have any friends to have his own bachelor's night and I feel bad about it. It's certainly a factor but I also don't feel the need to do something that's considered your last night of freedom. I'm not being shackled to Cas.

"Yeah, well, I want to do something."

"Oh," I say surprised.

"With you," he says quickly. "With you, obviously."

"The wedding's this Saturday," I tell him.

"Oh, shit, really? I thought it was next month."

I roll my eyes. He's really not as funny as he thinks he is, which is very funny apparently.

"Well, I thought I'd remind you since you usually need at least a week to plan something."

"Jokes on you because I already have everything planned." I look at him, waiting. "Oh, that's funny. Thats gold. You think I'm going to tell you? He who surprises me at least once a month with something? Yeah, no, you're just going to have to wait and see."

"Well, when is it? We have rehearsal dinner Friday night."

"I'm aware. But Friday from morning until then you're mine."

"I'm always yours," I say and Cas reaches out in the dark, finds my lips with his thumb and holds it there.

He says, "Not yet but soon."

I kiss his thumb. "No, always, Cas. Since the very first day."

Cas slides over from his pillow to mine, face so close our noses touch. "Thank you," he says. "For being a bridezilla. I know I joke about it, but you've been amazing. And I know our wedding day is going to make me cry. And will probably be the thing that kills me, honestly."

"Old age is going to be the thing that kills you," I say quickly. "Very old age. Guinness world record old age."

He laughs. "Just as long as you beat my Guinness world record."

"How about a joint world record? It'll be very The Notebook of us."

"See, now, that sounds really sweet but I'm nearly certain you're making fun of the Notebook. Which would be making fun of me since it's my favorite movie."

"What? No, I would never. Of a classic? Cas, how could you even suggest such a thing."

"Seeing as your favorite movie is Three Billboards I don't even know why I try."

"That was an excellent film."

"It was morbid as shit."

"But Woody."

"Yes, yes, Woody is excellent. He's also in Hunger Games. Significantly less morbid. Or Zombieland. Dark humor I can get behind."

"What about Anger Management? I like Anger Management and that's not morbid at all."

"What's your second favorite movie, Dres? Come on, name it for the court. They're all listening."

I huff. "It's not that I like morbid. I like good films."

"Manchester by the Sea, man. Could not get any darker if you tried. And let's not forget — out of all the DC and Marvel options out there. Your favorite is naturally Joker."

"Again. Another excellent film."

"I'm not arguing with that but it's darker than this bedroom."

"Casablanca's in my top ten and that's a romance."

"Yeah, I freaking blubbered like a baby when we watched it. It's freaking bleak."

"It's beautiful."

"And sad," he points out, jutting his chin so his nose smashes against mine.

"Most things are, Cas," I say maybe a bit too seriously.

He frowns. "Not us."

"We were once." Cas stares at me, unblinking in the darkness so I can just make out the whites of his eyes. I add, quietly, "I made you sad for five years."

"You'll make me happy for more," he says just as quietly. "And anyways," he adds his voice pitching animatedly. "I wasn't even really sad until I stopped writing you. So like one year of sadness."

"Well I was sad the whole time."

Cas pauses, going quiet again. And then he sighs, heavily, sitting up. His hands are on my chest, pushing me till I'm lying flat and he's on top. His elbow digs into my rib and I wheeze on a breath.

Cas leans down, face hovering above mine. "I want you to hear this and then this is the last time we'll ever talk about it again. And it won't be us burying it or pretending it didn't happen. It just simply bears no weight on where we go from here or who we are, okay? Say okay."

"Okay, Cas," I say.

"Thank you. Now you know that I forgive you. I know you know that. And my forgiveness, it absolves you, Dres. Because I'm the person you hurt and so I'm the person who gets to decide what is absolvable. And I also make the rules. Which means the way anyone else feels about it is irrelevant.

Including you. The thing you did was shitty but it's not the only reason why I was hurting. I hurt because I missed you. Because I was worried about you constantly. And you were the only person I wanted to be with that whole time. And everyone kept saying time heals everything and you'll move on and first loves never last. I kept waiting for the feelings to just dry up. And they didn't. That's what hurt, Dres. Not being with the person I knew I would spend my whole life loving."

Cas says things like this and I have to wonder who was I before I met him? Because I don't know. I don't remember what it's like to not be loved so completely and fully, for every version of myself, even the ones I'd like to bury, the ones I'd like to pretend don't exist. Cas loves me despite the ways I've hurt him. Cas loves me despite all the reasons he shouldn't.

And I don't feel undeserving of it. I feel like I'll spend my whole life trying to deserve it, instead.

"Those were my vows," Cas says. "So I guess I gotta rewrite them now. Although you could just pretend to be surprised."

I lean upwards, kissing him quiet. Kissing him in the most meaningful way I know how.

"So can I have a hint for Friday?" I ask as Cas tucks his head into my neck.

He will absolutely and one hundred percent fall asleep like this, lying on top of me, but I'm willing to allow it for tonight.

Cas mumbles, "You're going to need two pairs of shoes."

"That's a horrible hint," I say but Cas doesn't respond. He's already asleep.

Cas wakes us early Friday, but I was up late the night before working on desserts for the rehearsal dinner and our wedding cake, so I'm slow to rouse. Cas is not. He is all energy for seven in the morning, pulling at my limbs till he gets me out of bed and can lead the way to the shower, where he already has the water running.

The bathroom's full of steam but through it, I can make out Cas, who's bent over tugging his underwear off. That he's even wearing underwear is a feat because he usually goes to bed naked. He'd been asleep when I'd gotten back last night so that maybe explains why. Not wearing clothes to bed makes me nervous because what if something happens and I have to get out of the house fast and I'm naked? Like the house is on fire and I'm spending time looking for pants through all my dresser drawers. (I told Cas this once when he demanded I join him on this sleeping commando journey and he said that's why he leaves clothes strewn about so he doesn't have to waste time looking through his drawers) (I'd said right, that's why huh ?)

I'm caught up in watching him that he turns and pads over to me, reaching out towards my hips for my sweatpants. "You're so sleepy," he says quietly. "I'm going to have to wake you up."

He does wake me up, with a slow and soapy shower that is all exploring hands, like Cas and I have never touched before and have no idea what we like. He moans into the crook of my neck as his hand tries to wrap around the both of us and in twenty-four hours that sound will be mine. I'll be the only one to ever hear it again.

Cas dresses me in dark blue khaki shorts and a white polo that falls somewhere between sporty and casual. I wonder if we're doing brunch at a country club, or perhaps a rooftop place. It's early for brunch, though and I don't know that I would wear shorts for it. Spring has been sunny but mild, coasting in the seventies most days.

He hangs back in the closet, stuffing things into a duffle bag before he comes downstairs. Our luggage is already packed and waiting by the door and I've left printed notes on the fridge for Amelia, which mostly includes numbers for all the service people — my plumber, the HVAC guy, PSEG. As well as Delta and Charlie's vet and an emergency hotline for pets.

"I thought I needed two pairs of shoes?" I ask.

Cas nods. "You do. I've got them." He lifts the bag to show me. "You ready? We're taking your truck."

By that he means he's driving my truck, which is a sight I enjoy and is not something I'm complaining about.

The first place Cas stops at is the diner and there's a booth open in the back corner that we take. Our server comes by for drinks and we both order coffees before we open our menus. I'm pitching glances Cas's way while I look at the menu, trying and failing to find any nervous energy about him. Normally he's all nervous energy when he's got something planned but he's very calm now, easy going even.

He catches me looking and I go quickly, "What're you getting?"

"I think eggs and turkey bacon."

"Look at you. The turkey bacon convert."

"Yeah, you know, some random dude pulled me into his kitchen once when I was supposed to be working and made me breakfast with it and you could say it was love at first sight."

I blush at the memory and wonder how Cas was at all confused about how I felt when I was making him breakfast at work. That wasn't even remotely subtle.

My tone is serious when I say, "For you and the turkey bacon?"

"No, me and the random dude, obviously," Cas says just as serious.

"You're something ridiculous."

"I'm your something ridiculous," he says and then he goes, "What're you getting? And if you say oats, I'll punch you."

"What do you have against oats?"

"It's like porridge. It's sludge. Disgusting."

I'm not a diehard oats fan so I don't feel the need to defend it but I do make a mental note to convert Cas on oats, too. Probably with baked oats. He'd like those, I think.

"I think I want a crepe, maybe? I don't know."

"Well we'll be in France in five days. And then you could have a real crepe," Cas points out.

"True. Maybe I'll just do an omelette, then."

I get the omelette and Cas gets eggs scrambled with a side of bacon and toast. I ask for a bowl of fruit, too, and Cas picks out all the grapes and apple slices leaving me with the melon and kiwi. It's a quick breakfast. Normally Cas drags them out, eating slowly and interrupting the silence with work anecdotes. He doesn't now, eating quickly and even ushering me along as he checks his watch periodically. I'm on edge wondering what he's planned.

We have a joint account now and Cas gets his card out to pay. We put a percentage of our incomes into it and its meant for bills mainly, but if we go out together we'll use the card so neither of us feels like the other is constantly paying. Those were Cas's words. That I'm constantly paying for him (honestly I am and I'd keep doing it if he'd let me.)

Cas is quiet as he drives us out of town. We go one town over, and then another, until we're about twenty minutes from home. He's not driving by memory, which makes the commute a bit longer. I know his phones giving off directions and he keeps checking his watch where the notifications are coming in. Suddenly, he pulls over to the curb behind a white BMW. There's someone in the car and they immediately get out when Cas turns off the truck.

"What're we doing?" I ask, glancing at him.

"Come on," he says as a non-answer, hopping out. I get out too, just as he greets the woman who was in the car in front of us. She's pretty in a way you can't not notice, with short black hair that's both slick and wavy, reminding me of something out of the 1920s. She's dressed head to toe in white, with pants that billow in the breeze and a crisp, high necked blouse. She looks important and I don't recognize her at all.

"Dres," Cas says. "This is Janae. She's Prisha's partner." None of these names ring any bells. Cas seems to notice. "Prisha's one of my nurses."

"Oh, Nurse P. Right, right, I remember." I extend my hand to Janae who smiles at me warmly as she takes it. "It's a pleasure to meet you."

As we shake, Cas says, "Janae is a real estate agent."

My head darts his way, confused. He continues, "She's going to show us," he pauses, pointing over my shoulder behind me, "that house."

"Well like I told Calvin, I do have a few houses I can show you. All within these next few blocks. I know you have your heart set on this one but if it's not the one, there are plenty of other options that check your boxes."

Heart set on this one?

Check my boxes?

Moving into a house was always the plan but after we got engaged it became clear I couldn't go house-hunting, run two businesses, and plan a wedding so we'd decided that it would be a post-honeymoon thing. Particularly because Cas hated the process. Made it very clear he wanted nothing to do with looking at real estate and picking a place. He'd struggled to find himself an apartment, and a house was an even bigger undertaking.

So I'm thrown.

Which Cas must realize because he loops his arm through mine, leaning up towards my ear so he can say, "This probably makes absolutely no sense to you. But you were doing so much with the wedding, I wanted to help in some way."

"But you hate real estate shopping," I say still confused, still trying to catch up with this moment.

Janae is giving us space, scrolling through her phone as I look at the house that Cas has his heart set on. It's beautiful, without a doubt. It's older, looks like a three-story colonial with white clapboard siding, sandy brown trims and a red cobblestone foundation. The front lawn is large with flower beds below the wrap-around porch and there's an attached carport that I'm particularly fond of.

"I do hate real estate shopping," Cas admits. "But I love you. And Foer says loving someone means doing what you hate for them. But also Janae made it extremely easy. I wrote down everything I wanted and she snapped her fingers and voila."

"That's not exactly how it happened," she says with a laugh that is deep and booming. I've never met Prisha but I've heard a lot of stories about her. Cas says she's a five foot spitfire who can start a line in the dark (I have no idea what this means but it sounds badass.)

"Should I start my spiel?" Janae asks.

"Please do," Cas says. "I won't do it as well as you. All I remember is that this place has a pool."

Janae steps ahead of us, turning so her back is to the house. The sun shines down on her, hitting the high points of her face. Her complexion is dark but warm-toned so that the gold in her eye makeup makes her look regale. I wonder about her partner, what Prisha must look like beside her. She has the kind of commanding presence that tells me she's very successful in selling homes.

"This is one of the few remaining original colonials in this area. Built in 1890, but recently remodeled, the previous owners chose to keep most of the significant architectural components. It's seven thousand square feet with eight bedrooms and nine full baths."

I make a noise that causes her to pause. "I'm sorry, eight bedrooms?"

"Yes," she says eyes darting to Cas questioningly.

"Uhm, Dres," he says calmly turning towards me. "I don't know if you know this but we're having a ton of kids."

I balk. "Or enough to fill eight bedrooms, apparently."

"This is an excellent school district," Janae says.

"Although," Cas says stepping forward so he can turn and look at me. "If they go to the same private school I went to, they'll be a block away from Weston's. And like twelve minutes from the hospital. You can't beat that with a stick as you like to say."

"You've thought about this," I say my brain catching up with everything so slowly I suddenly feel like I've aged twenty years since getting out of the car.

"Extensively, yes. You plan the wedding, I plan the rest of our lives. Call it even." I stare at him, unable to utter a single coherent word. Cas flushes.

"Oh, the look you're giving me is full on indecent for the public, Dresden Gibson. Reign it in. There's company."

I try to but fail.

"Of course it's me being domestic," Cas mutters, shaking his head. "Of course. Why didn't I think of that like eight months ago? Okay, anyway, let's pick up where we left off. We're on a tight schedule."

My mouth drops. "There's more than this?"

"What do you think this is, amateur hour? Of course there's more. I'm competing with you."

Cas reaches out, grabbing my hand so he can pull me behind him as he walks up towards the front porch. Janae talks as we walk, pointing out the original wooden double front door that had been restored. It's a cherry wood with black brass knobs and leads into a small mudroom before opening to the entryway through a set of stained-glass French doors. To our left there's a small sitting room, in a sort of hexagonal shape with plenty of windows and natural light.

There's a stairwell beside the sitting room, also to the right of the front doors. The steps are wide and wooden, L-shaped with a landing before you can go all the way up. There's stained glass windows there — lots of stained glass, really. I'm failing to see what's been remodeled because everything looks original to the house.

To the left of the entry is another room. It's an airy study, again full of windows and lots of space. There's built in shelving, which I hone in on thinking about all of Cas's books currently taking up so much space pretty much everywhere in our house.

Cas goes, "Okay, yes, ooh, ahh, pretty study. I'm kind of crawling out of my skin for you to see this kitchen."

I elbow him. "Don't be rude."

"Oh, he's not," Janae says. "He vetoed so many houses because of the kitchen alone. I'm well aware of the importance of this one room."

I glare at him. "Cas."

He throws his hands up. "You're a diva about kitchens. Don't even pretend you're not."

I follow Janae and Cas out of the study back into the entry. Across the room there's a fireplace and beside it a narrow hallway. As we head that way, Janae tells us there's central air with gas heat, and radiators throughout. Cas makes a face at that and mumbles, "Bit of an eyesore but I'll survive."

I actually prefer radiators. It's basically steam heat. They're hardy and they really warm up a room without sucking all the moisture out of it. And since Cas prefers it to be a hundred degrees always, he'll actually end up appreciating it.

The kitchen is just beyond the hallway and it's huge. It's unreal. Janae and Cas keep walking but I stop, taking it all in.

"Oh wow," I say quietly, eyes sweeping across the room.

There's a huge island in the center. I think it's made of the original wood used throughout the rest of the house but every cabinet and counter has been painted a dark brown that's so close to black its hard to tell that they're not. This room has clearly been apart of the renovations. Maybe even the sole proprietor of the renovations. Counters run all along the back wall and on either side of the room. There's white cabinets and counter tops, tons of counter top space actually, and a farmhouse sink. This is my most ideal kitchen.

Cas says, "I learned a lot about kitchens in this process and I stand by the fact that I do not belong in one. There was another house in the running. But it had quartz countertops, which were pretty, right, but—"

"Not heat resistant," I say, interrupting him.

"Exactly and it just happened that during the same week I saw that place, you burned your hand on the hot pan you left on the counter."

"Look how attentive you are," I say joking but also not joking at all. Is this my wedding gift? This feels like my wedding gift and maybe even rolls over into a couple birthdays and Christmases, too.

"So we deep-sixed quartz. Marble was nice but the idea of sealing counters multiple times a year when I don't even know how to seal a counter? Miss me with that. So granite wins. Also please look at this walk-in pantry, Dres? Like as someone who isn't even a kitchen person I'm obsessed. I can't wait to tiktok-ify this room."

He swings open a door off of the kitchen, revealing the pantry. I go, "Have you been here before?"

"No, but I did the online tour thing and scoured the photos. I devoured them, really, so I pretty much know this house like the back of my hand."

Janae hasn't followed us into the pantry and Cas left the door cracked so I feel comfortable backing him up against the shelves.

"I'm gonna start amping up my domesticity? Domesticity? Is that a word? Either way I'm amping it. Because this," he runs a finger along my jaw, "your reaction? Oh, I want to burn it into my brain it's so good."

He drags his finger to my lip and I nip at it, which makes him moan softly. He drops his hand to my chest, pushing against me gently. "No, no. Don't do that. There's no time for distractions today. Tight schedule, like I said."

I place my hand over his, holding it there. "You want this place?"

"I want it, if you want it," he says quickly, the answer already there. "I want whatever will make you happy."

"You, in this house, with all of our kids. However many you want. And dogs, and cats, and chickens if you want chickens. That's what will make me happy."

Cas grins big. "Okay, wait, let's look at the rest of the house before you make a decision. I know the kitchen is freaking amazing. But there's one caveat and I had to really reconcile with myself to accept it."

Cas doesn't say what that caveat is, just leads the way out of the pantry. When we return Janae smiles at us like she didn't fully hear our whole conversation in there. I can't get over the kitchen. The large sink, the built-in double fridge. It's the kind of kitchen you dream of but it's usually just that — a dream. Out of reach. Not something that eventually becomes your reality.

There's a half bath in the kitchen and a hallway that leads outside to an enclosed patio. The dining room is off of this hallway, too, and it's large enough to host all of Cas's family and mine. At the other end of the kitchen is an archway to the living room with more windows to look out on the backyard. There's an office off of the living room and another stairwell, this one more narrow that leads both upstairs and down.

Janae asks us if we want to go up or down first. Cas insists on going up first, saying that I need to see the master bedroom. So we go up. There's nothing that particularly stands out about the master, at least not in a bad way, in a caveat kind of way. It's large, and bright, with plenty of closet space.

Cas grabs my arm and drags me into what I presume is the bathroom and—

"Oh," I say and then I laugh, and then I can't stop laughing.

"So you see my dilemma."

"This is actually really funny."

"Oh, is it Dres? Is it really?"

"Yeah, because on paper this house is perfect but given your propensity for," I pause, glancing behind me to see just how near Janae is but she's apparently waiting in the hallway, "shower sex, this is actually hysterical."

"Look, I'm not gonna let the fact there's two separate showers in this bathroom make us deep-six the whole house. But before we sign any paperwork I'm going to need you to sign a clause that states only one of these showers can be in use at a time."

"You've thought this through."

"Extensively, yes. Say you'll sign."

I bite back a grin. "What's in it for me? Maybe I want my own personal shower."

"Too bad, so sad, you're never showering alone again if I have any say."

Full disclosure, I have no interest in showering alone, anyway. But I do enjoy watching Cas get fired up about it. Two separate showers in one bathroom is a bit excessive. And the jacuzzi tub between the showers, while enticing, looks like a sex accident waiting to happen.

Cas catches me staring at it and grins slyly. "Oh yes."

"Oh no."

"Yes, yes, yes. Bathtub sex."

"That doesn't even sound sexy when you say it."

"Everything I say sounds sexy."

I can't even argue because with him, standing in this house that could very much be our house, yeah, everything he says does sound sexy.

Its another twenty-five minutes before we finish touring the whole estate. The basement has a gym, a bar, and game room. Outside there's the afore-mentioned underground pool with an attached hot tub. Its fenced off from the rest of the backyard, which, Cas points out, makes it toddler safe. But then I point that all our kids should learn to swim as soon as they can, anyway. The backyard is really impressive. There's a pool house and an outdoor kitchen and bar. But it's also a lot of house for only two people.

And it's like Cas is reading my mind because after we've told Janae we want it and we're sitting in my truck stewing over the fact we just put an (expensive) offer on an actual house, Cas goes, "Amelia should have her own bedroom here."

I look at him, startled and surprised. Amelia and him are close, that's no secret. And I love it because I'm close to Amelia and it matters to me how she feels about Cas but also how Cas feels about her. But this is still unexpected.

"Really?"

"Of course really. She's your sister, Dres. Plus, I feel like she needs breaks from city life so she'll be over often enough."

"I love you," I say and he laughs.

"Oh man. Oh god. This is my favorite day."

I smirk and say, "Well, tomorrow's my favorite day."

He wags a finger at me. "Alright. Stop being cute. Seriously. I can't get distracted."

I hold back my smile. "Right, right. On a strict schedule."

Forty minutes into the drive I'm able to recognize where we're headed. I don't say anything though, hiding my expression behind my hand as Cas silently takes us to the place we first hiked together.

It wasn't a popular trail when I'd taken him many years ago, but with social media being what it is, it's become pretty popular now. I've been back a few times and depending on the day and the time, the little parking lot may be full. Today it isn't, save for a station wagon and a truck parked near the e xit.

Cas parks at the other end and I get out before him, meeting him on his side of the truck. He's pushed his door open and has gotten out but he's turned towards the seat where he's rummaging in the duffle bag.

"I have socks and your hiking boots here," he's saying.

I press my hand against his ribs, turning him to face me so I can cradle his face and kiss him, hard, pushing my breath and my tongue into his mouth. He reacts in earnest, reaching up for a handful of my shirt, tugging me closer. I tilt his head, because it's not enough and I need to be closer to him somehow. And the only thing I can think is that he has to swallow me whole so I can live inside of him. Thats the only solution here.

Cas pulls away and I make a deep noise of discontent. He's smirking as he says, "Down boy. We don't have time for this yet."

The yet makes me hopeful.

"We should just skip the rehearsal dinner," I say.

He laughs. "Noooo, we can't just skip the rehearsal dinner." There's a playful roll of his eyes as he says it. Like I'm joking around, which I'm not. I'm so serious.

He realizes this and goes, "You spent all night on desserts for this thing. Are you kidding? Plus we've got the best Italian catering which is probably being prepared and packaged as we speak. Plus plus, what would we say to our family?"

"I think sorry rehearsal dinners cancelled so I can fuck Cas's brains out, see you at the wedding works."

Cas's mouth flops open. "God damn it, Dres. Way to put me between a rock and very, very hard place. Alas, I'm going to put my adult pants on and say the sex can wait, the rehearsal dinner cannot. Now come on."

Cas and I hike the same path all the way to where we rested last time. And when we get there, Cas unpacks lunch from the knapsack he bought with him. It's PB&J with the crust cut off. I often think that I'm the sentimental one, but Cas and I like to pass this role back and forth like a ball in an unending tennis match.

We make quick work of the trail back to the car afterwards. He's better at the hiking thing than he was six years ago and there's also no pouring rainstorm to make it difficult. There's also no hot and heavy car hooking up afterwards, either. Instead, we sit in traffic and make it with barely enough time to shower and pull ourselves together and get to the rehearsal dinner on time.

"You're late," Amelia says as greeting when we walk in.

So as close to on time as one can be when you're sharing a shower with Cas.

Cas, who looks so handsome it hurts if I stare too long. He always wears these unexpected suits that continuously makes me wonder where this style of his come from. A mark of LA? I don't know. It doesn't even matter. He's dressed in a white jacquard suit, high slim cut trousers and a fitted jacket over a silk black shirt. The pattern on the suit is so muted you can't notice it from a distance.

"So sorry," Cas exclaims a bit dramatically. "I was a bit busy pegging your brother."

"Cas," I snap, flushing as Amelia says, confused, "Wouldn't that just be regular sex for you?"

Cas ignores us both as he pushes ahead, saying, "So, drinks?"

I follow him to the bar thinking I'm definitely going to need some alcohol if these are jokes he's going to be telling all night.

CHAPTER SIX

C alvin Sumner

Dresden Gibson is in my hotel bed.

And it's exactly where he should be. Except he keeps trying to leave. I've got his forearm pinned under my elbow and my knee pressing into his hip. And he's laughing, but I'm so serious. He's not leaving.

"Cas," he's saying, all exaggerated sass. I know he wants to stay in this bed with me because why wouldn't he? I'm the best cuddler. "It's bad luck."

I let up my elbow, shifting over so both my arms are on his chest. He wraps his arms around me, his fingers strumming along my spine.

"I'm not letting you leave," I say with finality.

Dres gives me a look that's all challenge. With the sort of ease that's actually an annoying display of his strength, he grips my sides and lifts me in the air. My eyes balloon and I suck in a breath, bracing, for what I don't even know. He sets me down between his legs but I'm off balance and tip backwards.

"I'm marrying Thor," I say still sort of winded, staring up at the paneled ceiling. "I'm jealous of myself."

Dres swings his legs around me and gets out of bed, making his way to the bathroom. I roll onto my side to watch him. He's gotten more tattoos in the last six years. They run up the backs of his calves and thighs and over his hips. The only place left blank at this point is Dres's ass.

When I'd asked him about it, he'd said, "There's no tattoo I can really justify putting on my ass."

I had responded, mostly joking, "Other than my name. Yes, I agree."

I watch him through the open doorway as he cleans up and starts re-dressing. I roll off the bed and walk over, leaning against the doorframe so I can stare. Watching him dress is almost as good as watching him undress.

"Stay for one more hour," I say.

"It's almost midnight," he responds as he buttons his pants. He grabs a robe that's hanging on the door and holds it out to me. I roll my eyes but take it because it's a little chilly in the room.

"Did you see where my shirt went?" he asks passing me as he exits the bathroom.

It's by the couch. That's where I dropped it when I backed him up against it when we'd gotten to my room. I walk over and pick it up, holding it out h im.

"Ah," he says gratefully. I want to hang onto it, if only to be contrary, but I don't, letting him take it from my outstretched hand.

Dres finishes dressing before making his way to the door. I trail him sullenly. He's grinning as he faces me, which is kind of rude, considering.

I frown and he reaches out, hooking a finger into the belt loop of my robe so he can pull me close. Then he cradles my face, tipping it back. Our eyes meet.

"Don't pout," he says so I pout harder, making him laugh.

"You don't really believe that, right?" I ask.

"Believe what?"

"That it's bad luck."

He shakes his head. "I just like the tradition. I think it's romantic."

"Okay," I say quietly. "I'm not going to get any sleep tonight. But okay."

Dres pinches my cheek that's still resting between his palms. "I packed Zquil in your bag. Take two, turn the heat up in here, and you'll be out till morning."

I lift up towards him and he kisses me. It's a chaste kiss for us but, then, if it wasn't, Dres wouldn't be going to his room. Wherever that is. He refused to tell me lest I hold a stakeout. I'd thought about bribing the front desk, or just trying every door but it's a big hotel. Jack probably knows. He's somewhere in this hotel, too. Our whole wedding party is, actually. I could probably get it out of Amelia. I'm resigning myself to respecting Dres's w ishes, though.

He pulls away but rests his face against mine, breathing in deep. My eyes are open. His aren't. And he looks so at peace. Not a nerve in sight. I'm struck by how much I love him.

"Alright," I say with a huff. "Get out of here before I change my mind and cuff you to my bed."

The Zquil knocks me out.

I have an alarm set for eight but I'm up before it. I'm laying in bed on my phone, fixing some charts that have QA flags when there's a knock at my door. I get out of bed quickly, suspecting its Dres. He talked a big game about not seeing each other before the wedding, but he's a softie. Of course he couldn't stay away.

I open the door and turns out it's not Dres. It's room service. "I didn't order," I say confused. "I think you have the wrong room."

The attendant glances down at a receipt. "Room 322? Calvin Sumner?"

I nod unsurely. "Yeah, that's me."

I step out of the way and he pushes the cart into my room, making his way over to the balcony doors where there's a bistro table. I watch from a few feet away as he sets the table with plates and cutlery, and arranges the cart so most of the trays have had the lids removed. I have to tip him so I go for my wallet, not really sure how much I should be tipping. I'm not even sure where this food came from. I don't think breakfast was apart of the wedding package.

When I get back to him, he's holding out a card. "For you," he says.

I take it, slipping a twenty into his palm as I do. "Thanks," I say.

"Thank you, sir," he responds with a kind smile. "And congratulations." I must make a face because he adds, "On your wedding."

I flush. "Oh, right, thank you, yeah."

I wait till he's left before I sit at the table and open the letter. Immediately I recognize the soft tilt of Dres's handwriting.

Cas

There's going to be a lot of alcohol today and you know you're a lightweight. So carb load, as you like to say. I'll see you at the alter. I'll be the one still in awe this is my life and I get to spend the rest of it with you.

Dres

I'm grinning as I fumble for my phone. I start to call Dres but stop. He probably won't answer. I don't really know the pre-wedding rules. He can't see me before the ceremony, but does a phone call count?

I shoot him a text, instead.

[CAS] 8:06 A.M.: you need to stop bc if I love you anymore it's gonna be an uncontainable thing. I'll have to shove the excess into urine test cups and carry them around in a lunchbox like they're my specimen.

[CAS] 8:07 A.M.: aLSO hella rude I am not a lightweight I am simply efficient

[DRES] 8:09 A.M.: that's a horrifying way of saying why thank you husband-to-be of mine for sending me breakfast. You are so thoughtful and perfect in every way.

[CAS] 8:09 A.M.: See I would thank you properly but someone won't let me see them before the ceremony sooo

[CAS] 8:09 A.M.: I guess I'll just thank myself. Alone. On my own. With nothing but my imagination.

[CAS] 8:10 A.M.: And this fat dildo I bought.

[DRES] 8:11 A.M.: you're not smuggling that onto the plane

[CAS] 8:11 A.M.: dildo's are TSA approved

[DRES] 8:12 A.M.: what do you need that for

[CAS] 8:12 A.M.: I need it for when my husband is being stingy

[DRES] 8:12 A.M.: I'm not stingy. You're just insatiable.

[CAS] 8:12 A.M.: say that to my face! YOU WONT

[DRES] 8:14 A.M.: is this our first fight?

[CAS] 8:14 A.M.: pretty sure we had like three months of fights when I came home but sure we can call this a fight. It's getting me hot. Keep yelling at me.

[DRES] 8:14 A.M.: eat your breakfast

[CAS] 8:15 A.M.: I would much rather be eating you

[DRES] 8:15 A.M.: you're killing me

[CAS] 8:16 A.M.: we aim to please

[CAS] 8:16 A.M.: thats a 50 shades quote btw

[CAS] 8:16 A.M.: you kno my 50 shades jokes dont rly land when I have to tell you its a 50 shades quote

[CAS] 8:17 A.M.: standby there's a knock at my door.

[CAS] 8:17 A.M.: Is that you?

[CAS] 8:17 A.M.: Did I wear you down?

[CAS] 8:18 A.M.: Should I take my pants off

[DRES] 8:18 A.M.: ITS NOT ME

[CAS] 8:18 A.M.: OMG ITS NOT YOU ITS MY MOM

[DRES] 8:18 A.M.: PLEASE TELL ME YOU'RE WEARING YOUR PANTS

[CAS] 8:19 A.M.: PLZ KILL ME

My mom looks at me for no longer than three seconds before she says. "Are you being bad?"

"Why do you immediately assume I'm being bad?" I ask stepping out of the doorway to let her in.

I didn't take my pants off, thankfully but I did have to close my robe to hide the beginnings of a big one. My mother's presence is quickly killing the vibe, though.

"Because you have that face like you're being bad," she responds, walking over to the table with the courtesy-of-my-lovely-husband-to-be breakfast spread. It's nice to know my extremely horned up face looks like I'm up to no good to her. I should ask Dres what he thinks my face looks like.

She sits down and immediately helps herself to coffee, first, naturally. I take the seat next to her and say, "I'm trying to get Dres to break this don't see the groom before the ceremony thing."

"And how's that working for you?" she asks as she takes a plate and shovels some eggs onto it. She follows with fruit and toast and hands it to me.

"Why's everyone insisting on feeding me today?" I grumble and then add, "He's being ridiculously steadfast about not seeing me."

"He's way more traditional than I expected him to be about this," she responds. "Who's insisting on feeding you?"

"Dres," I say waving my hand across the table. "He sent all this to my room."

My mom's expression is so googly-eyed I think I should be concerned. She may run down the aisle and try to marry him.

"It's always been my dream, Cas, that you would find someone to take care of you like this. And before you say it, I know you don't need to be taken care of but it's just comforting to know that someone will."

"You've always liked Dres," I say with the slightest eye roll.

It's a good thing that she approves but it's also kind of annoying. Is there a man among of us who doesn't like Dres? Forget putting a ring on him, I need a collar and leash, or some handcuffs. Or a fat tattoo on his head that says Possession of Cas. Or all three.

"Because I never doubted for a second how much he loves you," she says. "It's always been clear to me. Maybe that's a mom thing."

"He does love me," I say, surprised. "Like a lot. It still blows my mind."

"It shouldn't," she responds, her tone sharp. I brace for the lecture but it doesn't come. Instead, she asks, "Are you nervous?"

I take a breath, push it out, and then respond confidently, "Not at all. I'm a little excited. But that's mostly because I've definitely got Dres's wedding gift beat."

She waits and when I don't say what my wedding gift is, she asks, "Do I want to know?"

"Probably not, no," I respond with a laugh.

"Alright, well I want you to make me a promise," she says suddenly.

"Dres and I have not talked baby names but maybe I can work Olivia into a middle name," I say.

She makes a surprised face and then a confused one. "No, that's not what I — you've talked about having kids?"

"Of course we have," I answer. "We're getting married. That's kind of something you want to be on the same page about."

She pauses thoughtfully then goes, her tone almost noncommittal, "And are you?"

I smirk. "Yes, we are. You will have yourself some grandchildren, rest assured. And they will 100% be going to Baxter, too. Which is great because then you can be in on carpool duty, too."

She reaches across the table and places her hand on mine, squeezing gently. "I'm so happy for you."

I turn my hand over so our palms are touching and squeeze back. "Okay, so what's the promise?"

"No more than three drinks today," she says.

I shake my head. "You're all acting like I'm some sort of alcoholic."

"Of course I don't think you're an alcoholic," she exclaims. "You don't drink enough to be an alcoholic, which is why you don't have any sort of tolerance."

"Alright, well, rest assured I don't intend to be going crazy on the alcohol. We've got a late flight and I don't want to arrive in London hungover. Or vomit on the plane. Not the most ideal way to begin a honeymoon."

"Are you excited for Europe?" she asks.

I grin. "Mom, I'm so excited, I may burst out of my skin. This feels like the highlight of my entire life."

She's grinning at me in a way that makes it seem like it may be the highlight of her entire life, too. It's always been like that with her. She put all of herself into loving me.

I know how to love because of her. It's the reason I'm able to give all of myself to Dres.

Dresden Gibson

Calvin Sumner is walking towards me.

And I'm walking towards him.

And this is the last time he'll just be Sumner and I'll just be Gibson.

Our wedding officiant stands between us. Sofia and Lily have already walked this path, dropping feathers that float around now in the wind. Maddox had walked down the center aisle, flanked by Charlie and Delta who are now seated next to Amelia in the front row. Cas has chosen the song and I half-recognize it. It feels familiar, like I've heard it somewhere else. It fits. Its right. All of it is. I've never felt more certain about where I'm supposed to be than I do right now.

Nobody is standing up front at the alter with us. Cas had insisted Jack, who's formally my best man, should be up there but I really did want it like this. It wasn't just for Cas's benefit. I didn't want to share my view of him with anyone else.

My view that is getting bigger and bigger the closer we move.

And then we're there, directly across from each other, standing before our family and friends. I can't resist it, can't fight the need to cup the back of his neck and pull him close so I can whisper into his ear, "Yours."

Cas moves, slotting our mouths quickly. It's a small kiss for Cas, but he manages to get his tongue in my mouth for a second before he pulls away, pressing our foreheads together as he says, "Mine."

"Don't cry," I whisper and he pulls away to glare at me as if to say I'm not going to cry but he's already starting, the corners of his eyes wet.

We shift back enough that there's a respectable amount of space between us and I look to George, our officiant. He quirks his eyebrow, posing the question are you ready? I nod.

"Welcome," he says, addressing the family and friends I've almost forgotten were present. "Please be seated."

I can't stop looking at Cas, am focused on remembering every detail of him in this moment. That he looks so beautiful it hurts, a good hurt, a reminder that I am so lucky to have him here with me.

"First, I'd like to begin by thanking each and every one of you for being here. It's no accident that you are here today, and each of you were invited to be here because you represent someone important in the individual and collective lives of Dresden Gibson and Calvin Sumner.

Marriage is perhaps the greatest and most challenging adventure of human relationships. No ceremony can create your marriage. Only you can do that—through love and patience, commitment and support, and most importantly, through forgiveness.

In learning to make the important things matter, we choose to let go of the rest. What this ceremony can do is witness and affirm the choice you made to stand together as life-mates and partners."

George says softly, "This is a day that will forever be remembered in the hearts of these two individuals."

This is a moment that will live on in my heart even after it has stopped beating. It is apart of the muscle, as essential to its function as the blood that rushes through it.

"And together you will divide all of life's sorrows, but you will multiply all of life's blessings."

Cas is crying heavier, the tears slipping down his cheeks. He wipes them hastily, giving me a pointed look, as if to say you didn't see that.

"Are you okay?" I mouth to him and he nods.

"There's only one cure for loving," George tells us and tells the room, his voice extending profoundly. "Love more."

George looks between us, his expression warm. He has only known Cas and I a short time, but he's looking at us like he has seen everything that makes us us and he believes in it just as much as we do.

"Dearly beloved and honored guests," he says next. "We are gathered here today to join Calvin and Dresden in the union of marriage. This contract is not to be entered into lightly, but thoughtfully and in earnest. The grooms have each prepared vows that they will now read."

I go to speak and Cas interrupts, saying, "Okay, I know we planned for you to say your vows first but I changed my mind."

Someone in the audience, his mom, I think, laughs.

"A lot of people think I'm dramatic," Cas says next and now a few people are laughing. Myself included. "Okay, so there's a good chance I'm very dramatic. Which is why when I say things like Dresden Gibson, you are my home, my life's source is rooted to you, you may think I'm exaggerating just a bit. But here's the thing. The thing is, Dres, you're like the solar system."

I inhale sharply, my eyes scanning over Cas's face, wondering just where he's going with this. It's been seven years since he said those exact words to me. And so much has changed — I've changed. But he knows me. He knows me better than anyone.

"But not just any solar system. You're my solar system. You're my moons and the planets I orbit. You're my North Star — you're every star. You're who I look up to and who I turn to in the night. And I love you with the certainty of the sun. As sure as it will rise at dawn, is as sure as I will love you. Every day. For all my days."

"I can't promise you the world, Cas," I say lowly, too low that maybe only Cas can hear me. I say louder, "I can't even promise you a slice of it. So I'm promising this instead: me. All of me. For as long as you'll have it."

"Forever," he says, cutting me off.

"Forever, then. Because I want it. I want as much time as I can have with you, and then I want even more. If I'm selfish in any area of my life, it is where it comes to you, Cas."

He grins, mumbling, "Okay, fifty."

I shake my head, mostly amused. "You keep interrupting."

"Well if you keep saying all these things to me, I'm going to massively interrupt," he practically screams.

"Cas," I hiss, my eyes darting sideways, mainly to the front row where his mom and grandparents are sitting.

"Oh, I forgot we had an audience," he says sheepishly.

"Oh we know," Amelia calls out.

Cas is flushing, so I make matters worse, stepping forward and leaning down towards his ear so I can say, "You are so beautiful, I have to remind myself that you're real. And in a few minutes, you won't just be real, you'll be really mine, too."

Cas turns his head, not to kiss me but to press the side of his nose against mine. His lips are so close he should be kissing me. But, instead, he says, "I've always been yours, Dres."

I want to kiss him. I want to kiss him so much and then more than kiss him. So I pull away, and step back, taking a slow breath to cool myself down.

"And now," George says after a moment, waiting, no doubt to see if Cas and I are going to go even further off script. "Calvin Sumner, do you take Dresden Gibson to be your lawful husband? Do you promise to love, honor, and protect him, forsaking all others, as long as you both shall live?"

Cas meets my gaze, steady and unwavering. "I do."

"And do you, Dresden Gibson, take Calvin Sumner to be your lawful husband? To love, honor, and protect him, forsaking all others, as long as you both shall live?"

"I do," I say and Cas moves, the way I half-expected him to, that I'm prepared to catch him because he's thrown himself into my arms, wrapping his arms around me tightly.

"I love you so much I can't stand it," he whispers into my neck. I can feel his hot tears on my skin, slipping past the collar of my shirt.

"Can you stand it for five more seconds so I can put a ring on your finger?" I ask quietly, just loud enough for him to hear me.

Cas laughs, the sound vibrating against my neck. "Yeah, okay," he says letting go of me.

He steps back so there's just enough space for our hands between us and wipes at his face. I feel choked up in the worst way, but we both can't be up here crying. Or maybe we could, but then I'm not sure who would see to the ceremony continuing.

George says, "And now for the rings."

I look out towards everyone for the first time. Cas's mom and mine sit together on one side. Cas's mom is in full tears, so I know where he gets it from. Across the aisle Amelia is on the end and his grandparents beside her. There's Jack and Jasmine. Atlas and Theo. Sofia and Lily and Maddox.

It winds me a bit, to know, that they're all here with us, bearing withness to this moment. It's been a long seven years. And I deserve this. I deserve this much happiness. I know I do. I feel it.

"Charlie, Delta," I call and they run up.

Cas crouches before them, cooing at them as he takes the ring boxes off their collars. "Good boys," I say softly, my voice cracking a bit. I'm coming undone, I think. Can feel my hold on composure breaking. "Go back. Go on ."

Amelia has to whistle but they turn back around and go back to her. "They're very well trained," George comments lightly and I huff on a laugh.

"All this guy," Cas says standing back up. He has the rings in his hand and holds it open to me so I can take his.

George says, addressing the room again, "Dres and Cas have these rings to represent the unbreakable circle of life and love. Please place them on each other's ring fingers and repeat after me."

Cas and I both repeat as we place our rings, "I give you this ring to serve as a memory of today and a promise of the future we will build together."

"And now by the power vested in me, it is my honor and delight to pronounce you partners for life. Go forth and live each day to the fullest. You may seal this declaration with a kiss."

I still have Cas's hand in mine, my thumb resting on his ring. I turn my palm into his, cupping his hand before I pull him towards me. My other hand snakes around his back, pressing firmly so he's arched against me.

"Kiss me and make it official," I tell him even though Cas certainly doesn't need to be told twice.

The music starts again and I can finally pinpoint the song. I know what it is.

Cas is grasping my face, holding me to him, kissing me with a furious intent that is just about to cross into absolutely indecent for the setting. Is probably already inappropriate for the children present.

The music heightens. I move my hand to the back of Cas's neck, pushing away enough to say, "I love you, Poe."

He's smiling and he's crying so I use my thumbs to brush the tears away. Cas reaches up, takes my hand and turns so he's facing down the aisle.

"I am so pleased to present the newlyweds, The Sumner-Gibson's."

"Here's to a long life, Finn," he says. I let him lead the way.

Calvin Sumner-Gibson

Dres. Dresden Gibson. Dresden Sumner-Gibson. Mine. Completely mine.

We walk down the aisle back towards the wedding hall, under the slew of flower petals being tossed by our guests. Dres is leading, or maybe I'm lagging, staring at his back, at his broad shoulders and his tapered hair cut. The top of his hair has been parted and swept off his face. The most handsome man I've ever seen. I knew it the moment I saw him, all those years ago. And even more beautiful now, with everything I know about him, with everything I love about him.

We pass the last row of guests, but Dres doesn't stop, leading the way into the wedding hall. The ceremony and reception are outside, so it's empty inside. I've got Dres's hand and I pull him towards the first door I see. It's a small sitting room, with two armchairs and no windows. Great.

Dres is grinning as he says my name. My full name. "Calvin Sumner-Gibson."

I reach up, pulling his face down to mine, kissing him open-mouthed, all air. Dres groans, turning his face away. "We shouldn't," he says.

"I just need a minute," I say quickly, frantic. My hearts racing and I feel. I feel overwhelmed. I feel like I can't think straight. "I just—."

I push him towards the chair and he falls into it, laughing. First, because he thinks this is something else than what it is, but then he gets a look at me and his expression changes, confused. I climb into his lap and wrap my arms around him, clinging to him.

"Oh," Dres says . "I thought."

"I know what you thought," I say, turning my face into his neck and breathing deeply. Dres tightens his arms around me and we stay like that, cradling each other for a few quiet minutes.

"That was the most intense thing," I say finally as my heart catches up with this moment. I feel better. Grounded. Being with him, apart from everyone else, is helping.

"I know," he says just as softly.

"I feel like after everything we've been through, like, I don't know. But somehow that was probably the most nervous and excited I've ever been at once? And I always thought that feeling would be reserved for the first time we fucked."

"So our wedding beats our first time, is what you're saying? Our wedding beats sex."

"Alright, don't be smug. I'm saying the feeling was more intense, yes," I respond with a roll of my eyes.

Dres leans back, cupping my face. He kisses one of my cheeks as he says, "Sumner," and then the other as he says, "Gibson."

"The hyphen's doing it for ya, huh," I tease. "I think someone's got a little bit of an ownership kink."

He tries not to smile but he can't help it. The hyphen is doing it. How fifty shades of him. There's a knock at the door, and I startle. Dres doesn't but he turns his head in the direction of the sound like he has x-ray vision. Or laser vision. He's giving the door the most lethal of looks.

"You both better be decent," comes Amelia's voice before she throws the door open.

"Shouldn't you have waited for us to say we are decent?" Dres asks.

Amelia looks at us quizzically. "What are you two doing? Is this part of the mating ritual?"

"I see comedy runs in the family," I say sliding out of Dres's lap. He sits up, giving Amelia a look that is all parts withering.

She throws her hands up. "Don't make that face. It may be your wedding day but you have responsibilities. The both of you do. So save it for the honey moon."

"Are they in there?" someone says behind Amelia and then Jack pushes past her to walk through the doorway. He looks from Dres, to me, and then back again. His expression is giving dad in the worst way.

"You guys literally can't wait twelve hours?"

I huff. "I'll have you know we're going to have to wait like twenty-four hours because we have a flight tonight."

That reality hits me hard. We're not going to have quality alone time until we get to London tomorrow, and even then we'll have to wait until we get to our hotel. Someone (Dres) did not think this through.

"We weren't doing anything," Dres says pointedly.

"Yeah right," Amelia says suspiciously.

"Your photographer is looking for you," Jack says next. "They need solos and then they want family photos and the sitter is coming to get the kids soon."

"What are you all doing?" Dolores calls as she walks in, brushing past Jack and Amelia. She stays at attention with her hands on her hips, eyes darting between Dres and me. "Do I even want to know?" Her gaze settles on Dres and I stifle a laugh.

"We weren't doing anything," he says again with emphasis this time.

"Right. Recall I have access to the cameras at Weston's and I'm well aware of yous twos' penchant for inappropriate time and place," she responds.

I gasp. "What?" I turn to look at Dres for confirmation and he shrugs his shoulders. "Oh my. You couldn't have told me that?"

"There aren't any cameras in the break room," he says. "Or the kitchen."

"The kitchen?" Amelia exclaims. "I'm never eating at Weston's again."

Jack makes a face. "Did I tell you about the sauna? Because I think I win."

"What about the sauna?" my mom asks as she joins us in what is now becoming entirely too small of a room with an entirely too inappropriate of a conversation for her.

"Nothing," I say quickly. There are some things mothers just don't need to know. Except Dres's mother. She can know everything and clearly does, has seemingly had an eyeful. "It's time for photos, right? We should go do t hat."

I hold my hands out to Dres, helping him out of the chair. He presses his hand to the small of my back as we follow everyone out of the room back into the entryway before stepping outside.

"So what's everyone else doing?" I ask.

"It's the cocktail hour," my mom answers. "They're getting drunk."

"Jealous," Amelia remarks from behind us as our photographers walk over.

"Can I steal the grooms for photos?"

"And I'll take the rest of the wedding party for your photos."

"Steal away," I say following Dres and one of the photographers away from the reception tent where everyone's gathered.

We're led down a cobbled path towards a decorated gazebo. It looks like something out of a fairytale with gauzy white ribbons and lots of cream-colored flowers. Their green stalks and leaves are a sharp contrast.

I can hear the camera shutter as we're walking and try not to let it affect my gait but it's starting to feel like I'm walking funny, too conscious of being photographed. Dres takes my hand, lacing our fingers.

Without looking at me he says, "Don't be nervous. They're just photos."

"Yeah, photos we're going to show our kids and that everyone's going to want to look at."

"Don't be nervous," he repeats, squeezing my hand.

We step into the gazebo and our photographer, Nina, directs us. We're back to back at first and then I'm instructed to turn, tapping on Dres's shoulder to get his attention. We're mimicking a first look, I think, but since I've already seen Dres, and married him, this is kind of difficult to fake.

And then I think I don't really want my wedding photos to be so staged. It's not us. So I scrap the idea and fling myself onto Dres's back. He is so unsuspecting we nearly go down and he has to throw an arm out, bracing on the banister of the gazebo.

"Cas," he exclaims, sounding winded. I can't respond, too busy laughing. "You're supposed to be taking this seriously."

"These are actually lovely," Nina calls to us.

"See, they're lovely," I say and then drop my head, kissing the side of Dres's neck. I bite it next and he groans, losing his balance so we both hit the ground. "Oh man," I say between the pain and laughter. "I thought you could handle that."

"Maybe when I was younger," Dres says holding his side.

"Shut up, you're not even old," I respond with a roll of my eyes. "Since I've got you down here, can you please tell me what you were thinking when you gave us no grace period between the wedding and the flight tonight?"

"How did I know you were going to harp on that?"

"When am I getting my wedding sex, Dres?"

"Oh my god, Cas, the photographer is right there. I am so sorry."

"Heard it all, seen it all," she says. "I can make these photos work, too, if one of you wants to move closer to the other."

Dres shifts onto his side beside me, propping himself up on an elbow so he can hover over me. "You get it tomorrow," he says reaching for my chin so he can tilt my face up. It's my favorite gesture of his. "Delayed gratification."

I'm ready to make a remark about how I've never been a delayed gratification kind of guy but Dres cuts me off, leaning down to kiss me. It's chaste, for the photo's sake I think, but I sneak some tongue in there because I can't not.

"Don't get ahead of yourself," he murmurs against my lips.

"I am who I am, Mr. Sumner-Gibson," I mumble back and he grins.

Dres gets up and helps me to my feet. "Can you get through the rest of these photos without being inappropriate?" he asks.

"That's very rude. Of course I can," I respond but honestly I'm not so sure.

Does Dres look even more devastating now that he's wearing a ring and my last name? Absolutely he does.

I need a place to channel all of my emotions, need the intimacy to solidify everything I feel so I can carry it better. Being with Dres is always good, but that's only part of the reason I want it. When we're together, that close, I feel like I have a place to put all my feelings. I get full on how much I love him and I can empty some of it into sex so it's not so heavy.

I didn't understand that for the longest. And maybe I still don't, not fully anyway. I just know that I can breathe easier afterwards. I can look at him without feeling like I'm going to crumble under everything I'm feeling. Sex has never been just sex with him.

Dresden Sumner-Gibson

After the photos, our family returns to the reception. Cas and I make the couple's entrance and everyone stands at their designated table to applaud us as we move towards our table at the center of the room. Once we're there, we sit down and the rest follow us except for our mothers.

"Thank you all for joining us on this momentous day," Dolores says. "We are so grateful to have you here to celebrate with us, especially after a long and devastating year. We understand the risk of being here and appreciate all of you for taking precaution."

"We ask that you join us in toasting the newlyweds," Olivia says next holding up a champagne flute. "To Dres and Cas."

Our guests hold up their glasses and repeat it back before drinking. Cas takes a sip from his glass but I'm parched and drink nearly the whole thing.

"Whoa there big guy," he says giving me a concerned look. "Two seconds into marriage and I'm already pushing you to alcoholism?"

"There's a lot of attention on us," I say. The fluttery feeling in my chest is definitely a symptom of that.

"Ugh, I know, it's almost like it's our wedding day or something," Cas says cheekily.

"Not funny," I say flatly.

"Did you eat today? I feel like you're getting hangry. Look the food's coming. Here, have some water." Cas pushes a glass my way and I take it. "I'm gonna see my grandparents," he says standing. "Don't be drunk when I get back."

"That's your thing," I say as he goes.

I'm nursing my glass of water, the feeling in my chest starting to ease when Dolores leans down over my shoulder and goes, "Do you feel any different?"

"Not really," I tell her. "Should I?"

She slides into the open chair beside me. It's Jack's spot. He's over by the bar with Jasmine. Their sitter was waiting for them after we finished family photos, so Atlas and Theo are gone, leaving Jack free to get "sloshed" as he put it.

Dolores goes, "Honestly, I don't think so. I think you married that boy the moment you laid eyes on him."

I choke on the water I was sipping, wiping my mouth before I say, "Excuse me?"

She laughs. "Can't tell if you think old age has soiled my memory or that I'm not sharp enough to notice things."

"No, I'm thinking what are you even talking about?"

Dolores's expression is knowing. "Five minutes into Cas working at Weston's and you were trying to feed him all the time."

I flush. "I was not."

"Maybe you're the one with the bad memory," she says. "Because every morning like clockwork you stood outside my office, asking me do you think he ate breakfast? And I'd be like did who eat breakfast? Cas you'd say all exasperated like I was just supposed to know. Every morning."

Now I'm really flushing. I honestly had forgotten about it. "He had those early practices. There was no way he was eating breakfast."

"You should've known right then how you felt. You always try to feed the people you love. I don't know, Amelia, is that a love language?"

Amelia looks up from her phone. "Is what a love language?"

"Feeding people," Dolores says the same time I say, "It's not."

Amelia laughs. "Mm, I think it falls under acts of service. Why are we talking about Dres's love language?"

I huff. It's not my love language. I don't have a love language. Love languages aren't even a real thing. And I definitely don't try to feed everyone and if it wasn't for me, Cas would be skin and bones because he can't even cook.

"There was one morning where you made Cas breakfast. You left me at the counter so you could feed him. You really think I wasn't wise to you's two's antics?"

Okay, so maybe I was feeding Cas as a way to express myself a little.

"Ooh, a trip down memory lane, I love it," Amelia goes. "Tell me more."

I grimace. "Or we could not."

"Cas used to walk around all starry eyed for you, Dres. It was adorable," Dolores says next.

"What about Cas?" Cas asks as he walks up, slipping back into his seat beside me. I drop my hand onto his knee and squeeze it.

"We're reminiscing," I say turning my head towards him as I add, "Apparently you walked around starry eyed for me."

"I did nothing of the sort," Cas exclaims, slapping my hand as I laugh.

His mom is seated beside him and turns away from Charles to say, "You most certainly did. Every single dinner. Dres did this. Dres did that. Did you know Dres can carry two trays at once? Did you know Dres has a tattoo of Morissey?"

I squeeze his knee again, raising an eyebrow at him as his face goes red. "Mom," he says. "There's some things that should be taken to the grave."

"No, please tell me more," I say.

Cas elbows me. "Okay, yeah so I was carrying a torch. Sue me."

Dolores interjects with, "You both carried torches. Cas's was just more obvious. I remember the day you two had your first date. Dres was so nervous."

"What," he exclaims. "You were?"

I refrain from responding. How am I being embarrassed about something that happened seven years ago?

Dolores is on a roll with the story telling. I've actually greatly underestimated her memory. "I walked in on you two dancing. It was adorable."

"Uhm, yeah, and you totally ruined our first kiss," Cas says.

I make a face. "She didn't walk in on our first kiss."

"Yeah but the potential was there. You were definitely going to kiss me. And then you got stage fright."

"I did not get stage fright."

"I can recall Cas here thinking that night was a one and done," his mom says. "He came home so moody. Oh the angst was oozing out of your pores."

"Alright, mom, chill," Cas says.

"Oh, I fully remember," I say, biting back a grin. Cas had been so sassy the following day. He'd quit. All because I'd gotten in my head and couldn't kiss him. It's crazy to think about how nervous I'd been to make that move.

"And now look at us," he says his voice low.

"Who would've thought it?" I say and Cas beams at me. He loves when I can make a reference from this day and age.

We're interrupted as the servers dole out the first course, slipping platters of warm pita, various hummus's and veggies onto the table. Cucumber, tomato, and feta salads follow the platters. The dinner menu has a heavy middle eastern nod, all thanks to Cas, who wastes no time digging in. There's spoons in the hummus to serve onto your own plate, but Cas has slid one of them in between us and is taking hefty scoops, alternating with pita and red pepper slices.

"Oh yeah buddy," he says catching my eye as he licks hummus off his thumb. "This is what you signed up for. Table manners be gone."

I roll my eyes. "You never had table manners."

"Hey, that's rude. I have excellent table manners."

"You eat like you've been starved your whole life."

"Maybe I was starved. In another life."

"Please don't start with the multiverse."

"It's real!"

"Fine, fine, it's real. I can't have this argument again."

"I know you're just agreeing with me to agree with me," he says moving on from the hummus to the salad. "But a win is a win."

I glance around our table and it seems like everyone's distracted enough that I can give Cas his wedding gift without all eyes on us. Cas is fully engrossed in his salad, humming as he eats. It hadn't even been a question on the dinner menu. I knew this would please him.

I reach into my suit jacket, removing the envelop from the breast pocket and hold it over Cas's plate, blocking him from dipping his fork back into the salad.

"Oh no," he says, shooting me a look. "Here we freaking go. What is it now? A timeshare in Bermuda?"

I don't say anything, waving the envelope so he'll take it. He does but not without saying, "Why do you always gotta do things..."

"It's your wedding gift. It's customary."

"You're my wedding gift," he retorts and I want to say he's joking but I'm fairly certain he's not. Maybe I should've booked our flights for tomorrow morning and gotten us a hotel tonight.

Cas opens the envelope and pulls the photo inside out. It's a polaroid of a very pregnant Australian Shepherd named Hope. I watch Cas's expression, the turn of his eyebrows telling me he's confused. He turns the photo around, checking the back for any hints before he looks at me.

"We're adopting a senior dog?" he asks.

"I don't think Hope would appreciate you calling her a senior dog. She's still in her litter-bearing years. In fact, Hope's days away from giving birth to Delta and Charlie's new sibling."

I expect excitement from Cas so naturally that's not what I get. His eyebrows go up and come together, making it look like he's about to cry. His voice cracks when he says, "You got me a puppy?"

I frown. "Wait — you're not supposed to cry."

"Dres, you got me a puppy," he repeats and it's loud enough that we're no longer having a private conversation.

Olivia leans over so she can look at us both, and says, "You got a puppy?"

Cas brushes his thumb under his eye and nods, holding the photo out to his mom. "She's giving birth to my puppy."

"Now that's a wonderful gift," she says. "You've always wanted a dog."

Cas shifts, pressing his shoulder against mine. I press back.

He goes, "This is perfect. But I'm going to top it."

I roll my eyes. "You don't have to top it."

"Sure I do," he says quickly. "I'm not starting this marriage letting you think you're more romantic than me."

I turn to look at him, then lean down biting his shoulder through his jacket. "Hate to break it to you, babe, but I am."

Calvin Sumner-Gibson

Dres thinks he's more romantic than me? Bull crap. I'll show him more romantic.

My wedding gift is scheduled before the cake and our first dance, just after dinner and speeches. It seems that everyone in the wedding party wants to say something. Jack, Amelia, my mom, Dolores, Amelia again (she's a bit drunk now.)

When it's finally time, I move to drag Dres away. "Come on," I say into his ear, pulling him out of the crowd.

"Where to?" he asks.

"I know you know it's a surprise," I chide, tugging him up the path back into the wedding hall. I'd quartered a room earlier and let the artists set up beforehand.

When I get to our door, I hold Dres in place outside it for a moment, staring at his curious expression, which quickly turns dubious.

"Is sex my gift?" he asks.

A hard laugh bursts out of me and I flush at the thought. "Sex would be my gift."

Dres grabs both my lapels and pulls me into him, brushing his jaw across my cheek so he can whisper in my ear, "Fucking you is always a gift, Cas."

A shiver rolls down my spine and I'll be damned if I don't press up against Dres so I can feel the hardness between his legs. I run my hand across his stomach, love-softened abs, starting a path down towards his belt when Dres grips my hand. "You're getting ahead of yourself."

"Always," I respond with a little roll of my eyes. "You know, it's always getting ahead and never getting head."

I feel Dres's chest shake with his laughter. "Is that what you want?"

"It's what I always want but we don't have time for that," I say with a huff. "I need to behave. And give you your gift. Come on."

I push Dres away, giving me enough space to turn the door handle and usher him inside. He takes up the doorway and I have to peak around him to see the two tables set up in the center of the room. They look like massage tables and there are ring lights facing them.

"What is this?" Dres asks glancing at me over his shoulder.

The two artists are hovering to the side, unpacking their kits. They're already wearing their gloves and masks. I had okay'd the sketch and now it was a matter of getting Dres on board.

"Well this is Helena and Rose. I believe you know them actually."'

He looks confused. "Yes but—."

"Uh huh?"

"Are you?"

"And you."

"Us both?"

"Matching, Dres," I say with a nod, pushing him towards the table.

"Matching tattoos?"

"Yes, babe, yes matching tattoos. Aren't you going to ask me the burning question?"

"The burning question?" he repeats, clearly still a little shocked.

I refrain from laughing. "Well given that you are already a walking mural..."

He gets it. "Where are we putting these?"

Leave it to me that I finally get Dres's pants off but I can't even touch him. For the last thirty minutes we've been face down on these tables while Helena and Rose work in tandem on their respective asscheek.

I say into the massage table, my voice muffled, "The idea, you know, came to me when I realized there was only one place left you hadn't tattooed."

"So what exactly are we getting?"

"Well I'm obviously branding you. With my Calvin seal."

"Cas."

"You'll see."

"Cas."

"What does it matter if I tell you now! We're too far gone."

Dres groans. "Is it a penis? Is it your penis?"

I try not to shake with my laughter. "Damn, that's actually a good idea. Is it too late to switch designs?"

Helena says in her gritty voice, "Since we're done, I'd say yes."

Rose helps me off the table and I do a slightly undignified waddle over to the full length mirror, holding my toga-towel in place. I'm staring at my reflection when Dres comes up beside me. He angles himself to look at his left asscheek, which lines our tattoos up since mine's on my right.

Considering it's my first tattoo and we were short for time, I didn't want anything huge. We both have the same outline of a lightsaber, modestly sized with fine line-work. Dres's is green and mine is blue. They're angled so if we pressed out hips together they'd touch at the tips.

Dres doesn't say anything at first. I give him exactly one minute to react before I panic. "If you hate it I will pay for laser. Or a cover-up piece. I bet Rose can turn this into someone's face or something."

Dres, still not having reacted at all, turns away from the mirror. "Can we have the room for a moment? There's an open bar. Feel free to help yourselves."

Rose chuckles. "Open bar? Say less."

Helena winks at me as she goes. It's a wink that says nicely done but by the way Dres has yet to respond I'm not so sure.

"Look, I know it's not really your tattoo style but—." I'm halted as he turns back to me and steps into my space. There's nothing but these half-assed makeshift toga's between us and that is simply not enough. "I thought," I try again as he puts his hand on my stomach and pushes me back. "I thought it was sentimental," I somehow manage to get out as he presses me against the wall between the mirror and a vanity.

I swallow, my throat unreasonably dry now. "Sentimental," I repeat even though Dres has completely stopped listening to me. He's dipped his head into the collar of my shirt and he clamps his teeth on my skin when I say, "Without being too—."

He jerks his head away suddenly, snapping, "Be quiet" as he kisses me, knocking my head back against the wall. It's an open-mouthed kiss, an anywhere-but-here kiss, hot and slow, lots of tongue, too much tongue for where we are with the little time we have. And honestly with what we're wearing or rather what we aren't. I can feel the cross-breeze on my dick as it opens my toga like a curtain.

I am nothing if not a person who needs some verbal confirmation, though. So I start to pull back but Dres beats me to it, tilting his chin so our heads are pushed together but our mouths are not. "I love it, Cas. I love it. It's perfect. Thank you. It's perfect."

He's out of breath, panting as he speaks.

That thing in my throat, that's been there all day, pulsates. It's a sharp twinge that shoots right up to my eyes. Everything about this day feels too tender to live through, like just by being here we are tearing holes in reality.

"I love you very much a lot," I whisper closing my eyes in an attempt to soak my tears back up.

"Very much a lot?"

"Too much. Like an uncontainable amount. Where does it go? Where can I put it out?"

He takes my hands, brings them to his face so I can feel the dampness on his cheeks. "Put it in me, Cas. Always, okay?"

I nod, pulling him in, kissing him quick. "Always."